MW00625364

"You are my happy ending. Everything else happening around us. It doesn't mean shit."

OTHER BOOKS BY

C.M. STUNICH

The Seven Wicked Series
First
Second
Third
Fourth
Fifth
Sixth
Seventh

Hard Rock Roots
Real Ugly
Get Bent
Tough Luck
Bad Day
Born Wrong
Dead Serious
Doll Face

Houses Novels
The House of Gray and Graves
The House of Hands and Hearts and Hair
The House of Sticks and Bones

The Huntswomen Trilogy
The Feed
The Hunt
The Throne

A Duet
Paint Me Beautiful
Color Me Pretty

Never
DID SAY

C.M. STUNICH

SARIAN ROYAL

Never Did Say
Copyright © C.M. Stunich

All rights reserved. Printed in the United States of America. No part of this book
may be used or reproduced in any manner whatsoever without written permission
except in the case of brief quotations embodied in critical articles or reviews.
For information address Sarian Royal Indie Publishing, 1863 Pioneer Pkwy. E Ste.
203, Springfield, OR 97477-3907.
www.sarianroyal.com

ISBN-10: 1938623916(pbk.)
ISBN-13: 978-1-938623-91-2(pbk.)

Optimus Princeps font © Manfred Klein
Conrad Veidt © Bumbayo Font Fabrik
Stock images © Shutterstock.com
Cover art and design © Amanda Carroll and Sarian Royal

The characters and events portrayed in this book are fictitious. Any similarity to
real persons, living or dead, businesses, or locales is coincidental and is not
intended by the author.

this book is dedicated to the Never ending well of love we all have inside of us.

even when you think it's run dry, there's always enough for another drop.

1

Ectopic pregnancy.

What the hell does that even mean? I hear the words like they're far away, floating in a distant universe, not meant for me but about me nonetheless.

Ectopic.

I roll the word around on my tongue, or at least I try to. Honestly, I don't think my mouth is moving at all. I do my best to turn over, but my body won't obey my commands, leaving me in an icy darkness that flickers at the edges. If the light's really trying to make its way in here, then it's going to have to fight twice as hard to get past all of my blackness.

So much blood.

I remember standing on the driveway with Zella and Noah, listening to things I never really wanted to hear and then … I was with Ty. Always with Ty. I will *always* be with Ty. *Unless, of course, I die here.* I think about that really hard. I mean, what else do I have to do? I can't move, can't speak, can't even ask what that word means. *Ectopic.* It means 'out of place' or something, right? It means something is where it shouldn't be. But what does that mean when paired with my pregnancy? The word ectopic sounds alien, like I have a little extraterrestrial baby inside of me. Only I know that's not true. I mean besides the ridiculousness of it – I'm too far beyond delirium to care about logic.

But this is Ty's baby. My baby. *Our* baby.

I groan and try to sit up again, but I'm still not fully present in my own body and it's freaking me out. If I die now, then Ty will die, too. I know that as surely as I know the earth is spinning on its axis. Ty and me, we're healing but we're not healed, not yet. Without each other, everything would just go to shit.

But that blood.

I remember the red between my legs, coating my thighs. I touched it with my hand and spread my fingers. Even in this in-between, I know what that means. It means trouble and heartache and me fucking up something as basic as pregnancy.

I moan again and fight against my eyelids. *Why do*

they have to be so heavy? I wonder, thrashing and trying to push myself up and out of this dark place. It's too dark here, not that kind of perfect dark that Ty and I make together, that kind where the stars flutter and rest and float high above us. I think of my sisters, of my son, but mostly I keep thinking about Ty. The kind of love we have is so rare that even if there is a heaven or another life after this one, it would take me a million tries just to find someone half as good as him. And even then, it still wouldn't be right.

"Ty," I whisper, and this time I know I'm really talking. My voice whispers from my throat, grating and so quiet I wonder if anyone could hear me over the other sounds in the room, the people talking and the machines beeping. But he does. Ty hears me.

"I'm right here, baby," he says, and I feel his ringed fingers close around mine, squeezing so tight I feel like my hand might break. But I don't care. I'd let him shatter me into pieces if he wanted to because I know he could always put me back together. "I'm right here, Never. Stay with me, okay? Baby, I need you. Little Noah needs you. You can make it through this."

I wonder why his voice sounds so sad, like he's pushing back tears, like I'm in a coffin instead of ... wherever it is that I am. *A hospital, I think. I'm in a hospital. My baby is dead. I'm dying, too.* And it's my own fault. Ty told me to go to the doctor and I refused, wanted to wait. I didn't listen and I'm being punished for it.

"I'm sorry, Ty," I warble, but my voice trails off and his hand slides from mine.

Consciousness fades, no matter how hard I try to hold

onto it.

I hate that I don't even have the energy to say goodbye.

2

Dreams flood my brain with harsh lines and colors that are too real, too familiar to be comforting. I watch them all from a third party perspective and I'm almost certain then, *certain,* that I'm dead. Why the fuck else would I have to watch my father die again, unless I'm already in hell?

In this dream – no, no, this *nightmare* – my copper hair hangs down my back and for the first two minutes, the first two minutes that Jade's father has his hands wrapped around my dad's neck, I fight. I scream and shout and claw at him, but I'm too young, too little to fight off a grown man with a vengeance. For the next six minutes, I sit down on the ground and I do nothing. And it's not because I don't want to, but because I *can't*. That feeling of helplessness was just one of the ingredients that led to an epic meltdown of a life, a life that I've only just recently gotten back. How cruel is fate? To watch me suffer for so long, give my body away like it meant nothing, only to have it taken away from me when I gave it in love?

My brain shifts and that strange light flickers at the edges again. I wonder, *do I go for it?* Do I give up and let it all fall away? I feel so weak right now, like the possibility of ever returning to my body is too remote to consider.

Fuck the light.

I know that's what Ty would say if he were here right now, if he were standing in this endless loop of memories and nightmares, his ringed hand holding tightly to mine.

I see myself then, sitting next to Ty at one of our Sexual Obsession Group meetings, in that leaky building with that stupid rug. I see Vanessa, the group leader, smiling at me as I reach up and touch my chip earring, the prize that promised that I did it, that I kept clean, that things would be okay.

Ty's face appears in my mind, slowly, like pieces of a puzzle being put together. I see that sweet, serious smile, that stupid nose ring of his, the piercing in his left brow. But mostly I see Ty's big brown eyes looking at me like I matter. That's all I've ever really wanted, you know? To matter. To live. To be loved.

With a gasp and a start, like a newborn baby taking its first breath, I wake up.

3

I've seen movies where women lose their babies. They come to slowly, blinking back tears and they always, always, always ask *what about my baby?* And then they wail uncontrollably when someone explains it to them.

This is not how I wake up.

After that first shock of energy, I hear distant voices and I feel people around me, even if I can't see them, but it doesn't last long. I end up drifting in and out of the room, aware that something terrible has happened to me, but unable to decide exactly what that is. When I finally stop floating and come to rest, the world settles heavily on my shoulders.

I'm conscious long before I open my eyes, filled with a sort of wonder that I'm still alive. There's nothing like the threat of oblivion to wake you up inside, make you realize that everything you've been worrying about – money, school, jobs, whatever – it means nothing. All that really matters is knowing who you are and knowing who you love. I love my sisters, my son, my Ty.

I know he's in the room because I can feel him. I think I'll always be able to, even when we're dead. We'd best buy plots next to one another because if my bones and his aren't able to mix together with the earth, then my spirit will be stuck to wander and search for the man whose smile changed my life. A morbid thought, one I've had before, yes, but I've just faced death, looked that bitch straight in the face and told her to fuck off. I deserve to be a little morbid.

The longer I lay there, the more I can feel. First, it's my face, then my arms, then my toes. As my body starts to wake up, I feel Ty's warmth pressed into my arm and I fight to lift my hand up, tangle my fingers in his hair.

As soon as I do, I open my eyes and find him raising his face to look into mine.

The grief and the fear in his eyes is more than enough to undo me and I soon feel the tears start to fall.

"I want a cigarette," I croak as Ty's eyes shimmer with tears and he lifts up a hand to cup the side of my face. He tries to smile at my ill timed joke, but the expression doesn't stick.

"Never," he whispers, his voice rough and unfocused, like it's been torn apart by sobs. "Oh my fucking God, Never." Ty leans in and presses his forehead against mine as liquid drips down both our faces, salty tears that I'm not even sure how to interpret, not yet. "I thought I was going to lose you," he whispers, echoing my own fears. I'm not afraid of dying though. No, that's not it. I'm afraid of losing this, of losing him.

"I'm sorry I killed your baby," I say, not even bothering to ask. I know. I can tell. That blood, that feeling of dizziness, the weird pain in my shoulder. Ty adjusts himself, sitting back so he can look me in the eyes, a very serious expression tightening his lips. His bracelets jingle and I close my eyes, the sound like music to my ears.

"We can make more babies, Never," he tells me and I purse my own lips tight to keep from sobbing. How can he say that to me? How can he act like I'm this important? Why? Why does he love me so much?

"I screwed up, Ty," I whisper hoarsely and he shakes his head. But I'm not done. "I screwed up. If I'd listened to you, gone to the doctor, this wouldn't have happened. I can't even have a baby right, Ty. That's something I should be able to do, at the very least. Even my bitch mom can do it. Why do I keep messing up? Why? Why?"

Ty's standing up now, scooting me over gently, and I realize that even though I can feel my limbs, my body, I can't really *feel* anything. I must be hopped up on lots of painkillers. My husband, my soul mate, he moves me just enough that he can climb onto the bed next to me, lay his warm body against mine. He's half hanging off, but I don't care. He doesn't seem to either. Ty tucks my head under his chin and holds me as tight as he can without hurting me.

"You didn't mess up, Never," he says softly. I think Ty's shaking and his voice still doesn't sound right. If he's that scared, things must've been pretty bad. I had no idea miscarriages were this big of a deal. My mom's claimed to have three separate miscarriages, one of them while she was waitressing at the pancake joint. You know, that one everyone used to go to, but that shut down years ago. She said she took a quick visit to the toilet and got back to it. Knowing my mother's work ethic, I doubt it. Besides, she's a bitch and a liar, too, but I guess I'd somehow let her words become my truth. Miscarriage, no big deal.

"I killed our baby," I say, but Ty is already shushing me with his lips against my hair. I brush him off and try to pull away, but apparently I'm not entirely in control of myself. My body rails against the effort and stays put. "And what's an ectopic pregnancy, Ty?"

Tyson Monroe McCabe stiffens beside me, his breath hitching sharply.

"You say you killed our baby, but that isn't true, Never. In all reality, I almost killed you."

His words trail off until I have to strain to hear them. *Killed me? How?* I ask him just that, but Ty is burrowing into my neck and breathing deep, like he's trying to memorize my scent. If he smells like cloves and tobacco and beautiful darkness, I wonder what I smell like? Antiseptic? Blood? Do I still smell like blood?

I try to push the covers back, but Ty curls his ringed fingers around my hand, covering up the blue and silver, the red and gold, of the rings he gave me.

"An ectopic pregnancy is when the baby grows inside the fallopian tube instead of the uterus, Never," Ty says, his voice still a whisper. I stare at the door to the hallway, letting the information sink in, wondering where my sisters are. I'd have expected to find Beth here, wailing and leaning over me, peering into my eyes and acting like she knows better than the doctors. "The cramps, the dizziness, the spotting ... " Ty shivers and sucks in a sharp breath. "Those are all signs. I should have done better by you, Nevs. I should have made you go to the doctor and then they might've seen it. You ... you almost died. Your fallopian tube ruptured, baby. You went into shock; you were bleeding from the *inside*."

I don't know what to say to that, how to feel.

"I've been bleeding on the inside since my dad died, Ty," I tell him as more salty tears drip down my face. "I'm used to it." I look over at him, watch his eyes, the shadows dancing inside of them, and I almost wish I had died. Who am I to make him feel like this? I'm supposed to make Ty's tortured life better, not worse.

"It's my fault. I almost killed you."

"What?" I snap, getting angry at him because I don't know what else to do, how to feel. "Because you came inside of me? Because you didn't put a condom on? Because you didn't tie me up and *force* me to go to the doctor? Tyson Monroe Ross-McCabe, I don't know what kind of woman you think you fell in love with, but have you ever tried to *force* me to do anything? It never really works out all that well."

Ty smiles at me, but his dimples don't show, so I know he's faking it. Unfortunately, I don't have time to grill him about it because the door opens and a doctor steps inside. She's young, pretty, her eyes sharp as thorns and her fingers long, curled around the edge of the pocket on her lab coat. When she sees Ty lying on the bed next to me, she purses her lips and gives him a look.

He glares back at her, and crosses his arms over his chest. If she tries to get him to move, she'll be in a for a real fight. Just like I can't be forced to do anything I don't want, Ty won't leave my side. Not while he's still breathing anyway.

"Well," the doctor says, stepping forward and checking some of the equipment by my side. I don't know what any of it does, or what the numbers mean, so I don't pay much attention. I focus instead on the black and orange butterfly that graces Ty's knuckles. *We lost our baby, but I'm still alive. And I ... I didn't really want another baby anyway, right?* I try not to feel bad for thinking that, but I do. I really, truly do. Ty and I had started talking names; he bought me that stupid skeleton T-shirt. I blink back a quick burst of tears and put my hand on Ty's bicep, hopefully to keep him from saying something stupid. Doesn't work. This is, of course, the same guy who walked into my class in the middle of a lecture with a cup of coffee and a commentary about penises. "We don't generally abdicate the sharing of hospital beds."

"I don't generally give a fuck about that. This woman is my life. Shit, she's more than just that. She's my everything, and I am not fucking moving."

Ty's words are a comfort, even if they are riddled with the F-bomb. His curses are like mini declarations, each one a testament to the amount and strength of his feelings. He's so passionate that the only way he can communicate right is to pepper his sentences with expletives.

"We don't generally abdicate the sharing of hospital beds," the doctor repeats, and I feel Ty stiffen, "but you've been through quite enough as it is, I think." The doctor moves over to the bedside and looks closely at the pair of us, at me and Ty. I wonder what she's thinking, if she thinks we're just two dumb kids who made a stupid mistake, if Ty is some loser of the month, a boyfriend who's in the door just as fast as he'll be out. I glare at her just in case. Can't help it, it's what I'm used to. Besides, when I had Little Noah, I saw the looks the nurses gave me. They can all go fuck themselves. I might have black and orange hair, and Ty might have tattoos for days, but we're actually married. Fancy that, a Regali girl married and having babies with her husband? There must be miracles in this world.

"I want a fucking cigarette," I say, just because I feel tumultuous and ornery in that moment. The doctor looks so put together while I feel like I'm falling apart. She's educated and pretty and young, and I watch with narrowed eyes as she shakes her head at me.

"My name is Doctor Pradhan," she continues, pretending I didn't say anything. I simply cross my arms over my chest, mimicking Ty's pose as we wait to hear whatever it is this woman has to say. "And I don't think you should be having a cigarette anytime soon."

"Why?" I ask, feeling a sharp break in my chest, like

my heart is cleaving in two. Hasn't life given me enough shit? Why can't I just be miserable and pregnant like everybody else? But no. I have to be one in a million, a girl whose father was murdered before her eyes, who lost her family to untruths and ignorance, who had an egg implant in the wrong place and nearly bled to death. "I'm not pregnant anymore, am I?"

"That's the reason I came to see you, Mrs. McCabe" the doctor says, glancing at Ty. "Mr. McCabe." *Okay, so at least she knows he's my husband. At least there's that. The world isn't totally fucked.*

"It's Ross-McCabe," I blurt and glance over to see a small smile on Ty's lips. He probably filled out the paperwork. Figures. Neither of us have legally changed our names, so I guess we can have this debate later. I'm pretty sure I'll get my way. Little Noah's birth certificate says *Ross-McCabe* on it anyway.

"Well, Mrs. Ross-McCabe, I have some good news for you."

Ty and I exchange a look. Good news is rare in our world. Or at least, it was until we found each other. I'm not sure what to think anymore.

"This is, to be quite honest with you, a one in a million chance." The doctor pauses and thinks for a moment, her dark hair glossy beneath the fluorescent lights that shine from overhead. "Actually, it's about a one in thirty-thousand chance. Never, your child had a twin."

"A twin?" I echo, glancing over at Ty whose dark brows are raised in surprise. Figures. The man is fertile enough to impregnate with a mere glance. Of course there'd be twins. But I don't see how this is good news.

If anything, it's even more tragic. Twins. Two dead babies. I cringe.

"Mrs.," the doctor trails off and decides it might be easier to continue using my first name. "Never, the second fetus is viable."

"And what the fuck does that mean, exactly?" Ty says, sitting up. One of his boots hits the floor with a loud slap.

"It means," the doctor says, smiling for the first time, "that you're having a baby."

4

"Are you happy, Nev?" Ty asks, still lying on the hospital bed with me, brushing my hair back with ringed fingers. His breath is warm on my neck, a comfort I sorely need right now. I'm not ashamed to say that after Doctor Pradhan left, I cried until my face hurt. It's still the only part of my body I can really *feel;* even my heart has gone a little numb.

I twist my fingers around his left hand, the one that's

bare of jewelry but decorated all the same, colored with butterflies whose wings dance and flutter as he adjusts his arm to give me a better grip.

"You asked me that before," I whisper, my voice still not entirely my own. It's too rough, too broken, and I don't want to feel that way anymore. I look up, at the sterility of the room, at the flowers in the corner. Each bouquet's from a different sister – there's even one from my infant son. I smile because I know my family can't afford flowers like that, and I sure as shit know Little Noah didn't pick out a Christmas bouquet. *Thank you, Noah Scott,* I think as I try to figure out how to answer Ty's question. "Last time, I said I was scared." Ty stays silent, but he doesn't stop stroking my hair, doesn't pull away. "This time ... " I trail off as the fingers on my right hand run across the white sheets, across my belly. I've just had a ... a what the fuck was it called? A *salpingectomy.* It's a procedure where part of the fallopian tube – the part that Ty's baby, my baby, where she latched onto – is removed. Luckily (or not) for me, the surgeon was able to reconnect the remaining segments. This means that my chances of getting pregnant in the future are still good. Isn't that nice? "This time," I repeat, because I'm still at a loss for words. "This time, you stomped into the hallway and told a frightened nurse to get your wife a fucking Jell-o cup."

I laugh a little, but the sensation's too weird with all of these drugs in me. It makes me wonder why I've complained all these years about the hurt, the pain. Without it, life is almost ... well, it's almost like this hospital room. White, sterile, impersonal. Now, I'm not saying I like to hurt; nobody does. I just think a little pain is okay, that it builds character. At the very least, I hope that's true because then it means that Ty and me, we've got character in spades.

Ty chuckles softly, but the sound is reserved, too reserved for him.

"Don't you fucking do that," I snap and he leans back just enough to cock his eyebrow at me. Our eyes meet and mine instantly fill with tears. Not sure why, but they do. Let's call it hormones, okay? "You don't get to mope around and be sad, and you really, really, really don't get to blame yourself, Tyson." He cringes a little when I say his full name and pushes up into a sitting position, one leg dangling over the edge of the bed. He's since taken his boots off, revealing a very disturbing pair of reindeer socks that he says he got from Beth. Hmm.

I run my hands over my tummy again and Ty helps me pull back the sheets to get a look, lifting up my hospital gown with a naughty grin that doesn't quite reach his eyes. He's trying to be his normal self, but the terror that still lingers in his gaze is awe inspiring.

"You mean, I can't blame myself or you'll stop letting me peep under your dress?" I give Ty a raised brow of my own, but as soon as he sees the scars on my belly, his entire demeanor changes, even the false humor he's been using as a shield drops by the wayside. I watch as a million emotions take over and release him, as he drags his hands down his face and crinkles up his brows. "Oh, baby."

I look at the scars for the third time since the doctor left, at the three little puncture wounds. There's one on either side of my belly button and another below it. Apparently, this is called laparoscopy, and it's a fairly noninvasive procedure. Instead of gutting me from hip to hip, making a little smiling scar across my belly, I got these. Looking at them now, it's hard to believe that such a small thing almost killed me, that I almost bled to death from the inside.

"God, Never," Ty says, my heart breaking at the sound of anguish in his voice. He leans over, putting his head against my breasts, and lets me run my fingers through his hair. "I did this to you. Me. This was me."

"Ty," I say, because I can't let him take this on his shoulders, can't stand to see the happiness that we've built so painstakingly get flushed down the toilet. "You heard the doctor: smoking greatly increases your risk of having an ectopic pregnancy. And come on, let's be honest, we both have a problem."

"But I ... I should've been more responsible," he says, his voice taking on this hard edge, one that scares the ever living shit out of me. Ty raises his face, and his expression is dark, the darkest I've seen since that day we got our test results back, when we both sweated and shook and stared at those pages like our fate was written in blood. And you know what? It was. It really was. But I saw then that I would live, and so live I will. But in order to do that, I need Ty to stay with me. "We both knew you didn't want another baby and Never, I'm good at that."

"At making babies?" I ask, trying to force a smile. Ty's having none of it. He stands up and puts his hands on his lower back, turning in a tight circle and taking deep breaths, like he's about to explode. His tight black T-shirt clings to his sweaty chest as he shakes his head at me.

"I'm good at making sure I *don't* make babies. I've never gotten anyone pregnant before, not once. And when it counts? When I know you're already scared of Little Noah, I fail you. I put you through this shit."

I frown and try to stand up, to throw my stupid white hospital blankets back so I can get up in Ty's face. It's hard to argue with someone when your body is strapped to machines, confined to a stupid uncomfortable metal bed.

Ty's there in an instant, holding me back with firm but gentle fingers, looking down at me with pursed lips and that look again, that one that says he's so scared he could probably shit his fucking pants.

"Ty, *we* did this together. I was just as much a part of getting pregnant as you were."

"I'm supposed to protect you, Never." He touches his ringed hand to his chest, bracelets jingling. "I'm supposed to take care of you. That's my reason for fucking living. It's my job as a man."

"Huh," I snort, shaking my head and trying to pull my arms from his grip. "With all of your wise wizard shit, and your raging feminism, I would've thought you were smarter than that. We take care of each other, Ty. We protect *each other.*" Ty finally lets me go and I touch my fingers gently to my belly. It's still flat, but I know it won't be for long. He follows the motion and then locks eyes with me.

"You never finished what you were going to say, if you were happy or not."

I nod and take a deep breath because I'm still in pieces and I'm still not entirely certain that I know how to feel, but one thing remains the same: Ty is my twisted, tortured, other half. We are two parts of one whole, and that will never change.

"This time," I repeat, "this time, I'm still scared, but I'm grateful to be alive, to be with you. I'm grateful there's an *us* that's capable of fucking up. Besides, you heard the doctor, we have a one in thirty thousand baby that's probably got copper hair and hazel eyes. When I passed out, I never thought I'd wake up. To be able to sit here, look at you, know that I really will see my son and my sisters again, yes, I am happy." I cross my arms over my chest. "And don't you dare fucking doubt it for a second."

5

Ty and I don't really get a chance to finish our conversation because, like a flock of copper haired seagulls, my sisters descend on me, squawking and flapping their wings. Apparently, I've slept through Christmas. *I ruined a holiday – like mother, like daughter.* I brush that thought away because it's not helping and I know it's not true. I mean, maybe me being in the hospital *did* ruin Christmas, but it wasn't because of a malicious neglect and disregard for others. *I hate you, Angelica.* Instead of having my mother by my side, petting my hair and whispering that everything's going to be okay, I have Beth. And you know what? I'm glad, thrilled even. Beth is the mother I never knew I had, the glue that holds this family together. Without her, I'm sure my little sisters would be scattered across so many foster homes. Instead, they're all standing in my hospital room.

Well, all except one.

I don't see Jade anywhere, but I don't have time to focus on that because there are too many other faces, too many other voices. I watch as Ty takes our baby in his inked arms, holds him tight to his chest and breathes deep. His eyes close and his bracelets sing a soft soliloquy to an audience of one.

"I'm sorry we weren't here when you woke up," Beth says, getting all red-faced and puffy. She's still wearing pajamas and her hair is piled on top of her head in a messy bun. She didn't even wait to get dressed when she heard I was awake, didn't even waste a single second to put on a bra before she shoved everyone in the car and rushed over here. I put my knuckles in my mouth and bite down to keep from crying again. For five years, I missed my sisters like I was missing a piece of my heart. And now here we are together again. "We took shifts for the first two days, but I felt like the kids should have a Christmas, and Ty wanted some alone time with you … "

"You don't have to explain," I say, glancing at the doorway, at Zella's tearstained face. She's got her hands wrapped around the doorway, half in and half out. I can see in her hazel eyes the need for forgiveness, but I don't feel like she should even have to ask. What happened on the driveway was a necessary evil, and I can only hope that she and Noah have worked things out. Based on their distance from one another, I don't think that's happened yet. He stands in the corner by the flowers, blonde hair like spun sunshine, all tangled up and mussy. Honestly, I have no idea what time it is, but based on the outfits in this room, it must be pretty damn early. "I'm just glad you're here."

Beth nods and then bites at her lower lip for a minute, pausing to toss the evil eye at the younger kids. The look itself is enough to effectively pin them in the corner with Noah until they're given permission to approach my bedside again.

"I called Mom," she says and we both cringe. I shake my head; I don't want to know. Apparently Beth doesn't get it and decides to tell me anyway. "She said she was sorry for your loss." I snap my attention back to my sister, giving her a look that says I'm not buying what she's selling.

"There's no way in hell that the egg donor said anything like that," I snarl and Beth's eyes tear up again. I don't mean to get aggressive with her, and I know she's stretched thin, but I won't let her lie to me either. Even though I know my mom is like this, even though I've promised to cut her off, her slights still hurt. Maybe they always will? "What did she really say, Beth?"

My sister fidgets for a moment and takes a deep breath, but in an instant, my anger washes away and I forget all about my mother. Ty is approaching with my son in his arms, and my heart starts to flutter like a trapped butterfly.

I sit up suddenly, struggling to get into a good

position to hold him. Beth helps me fluff my pillows as sweat pours down the sides of my face and my hands get all moist. The first thing I wanted to do when Beth carried him in here was hold him, but my sisters surrounded me and Mini McCabe ended up being handed off to Ty. And that was fine, good, great even, because I know Ty needs him, too, that Ty lost a child, too. That he almost lost me.

My eyes lock onto my son.

But now.

Now.

I take a deep breath as Ty pauses next to me, and my hands start to shake. I think he notices because he reaches down with his left hand and squeezes my arm softly, drawing my attention back to him. At least his face looks better now, calmer. I can only pray he's going to listen to the words I had to say.

"Everything okay, baby?" he asks me as our gazes meet. Without having to ask aloud if I'm ready, Ty knows, and he very gingerly puts Mini McCabe in my arms. I pretend like the moment is no big deal, shoving back yet another fresh set of tears through sheer force of will.

If losing the promise of a child isn't enough to make me appreciate what I have, then I'm no better than my mother. But I am. I know I am.

I cuddle Mini McCabe like I've never done before, hold him tight to me and breathe deep. Did my mother ever hold me like this, care about me like this? It's hard to say. I look up at Ty and see a warmness there, almost a sense of relief. I want him to know that any negative thoughts that might be showing on my face right now having nothing to do with my son. I think he already knows that, but I say it anyway.

"My mom," I mutter, looking down at Ty's child, at the dark hair on his head, the hazel eyes, the goofy smile. *This is just a stumble, not a fall,* I tell myself, and I hope that somehow, my baby can feel my determination through our connection. I hold him close and sigh, beyond ready to hear whatever it is that my mother's done now.

"What the fuck does that bitch want?" Ty says, putting a cigarette between his lips out of habit. He realizes what he's doing right away and clutches it between two fingers, giving it a longing gaze before chucking it into the trash near his feet. A moment later, the entire pack is gone, lying in a sterile stainless steel coffin. We both exchange a meaningful look.

"Apparently not her own daughter," Beth says, giving Zella a look. She tries to motion my sister forward, but instead, Zella turns and disappears into the hallway. "She ... " Beth looks so uncomfortable that I almost tell her to forget it. "She's at a folk music concert right now." I snort. Of course she is, probably working real hard at getting pregnant again. The sad part is, she knows that no matter how many kids she manages to squeeze out, that my sister will always take care of them. There are no repercussions for that bitch's actions. "She says she's sorry you lost your baby, but maybe this'll teach you a lesson."

Ty growls low in his throat and I feel my fingers tightening around my son's ugly little floral one-piece. Poor guy. I take back what I said: Mini McCabe really does look best when his father dresses him, zombie, pirate, and Sasquatch costumes aside.

"It's okay," I say, before Beth can start crying or Ty decides to go rogue and search Angelica out. "It's fine. I cut her off a long time ago. She doesn't matter anymore." I look around at my husband and my sisters, at the ex I never really wanted to leave behind, and then down at my baby. A big breath fills my lungs as I struggle to find the courage to look up into my sister's face again. "Beth, my baby had a twin," I say and she wrinkles her eyebrows in confusion. "She had a twin who found out exactly where she was supposed to be." *May we all be so lucky.* "So ... I'm still pregnant. I'm still having a baby. And this," I sweep my hand out to indicate the room and the people in it. "This is all that matters."

6

"No sex for six weeks," Ty McCabe repeats as we snuggle in the back of my sister's minivan. My belly hurts, despite the painkillers, but I don't care. I'm so happy to be out of that hospital that I'd do anything, suffer anything. I stroke my hand up the inner leg of Ty's jeans, and he reaches out to capture my fingers, bringing them to his lips for a kiss. I shudder at the touch and lean even further into him. "Six weeks, sweets," he says firmly, resting his chin atop my head.

A strange sense of déjà vu washes over me then, a memory of sitting beside Ty on a bus as we made our way from California to the middle of Butt Fuck Nowhere, Mississippi. It may very well have been the best decision I ever made. Well, other than deciding to marry Ty McCabe.

"What ever will we do?" I ask, loving that my lack of sex means he's also abstaining. It's not just my sex life anymore, or his, it's *ours*. I am the only woman Ty McCabe is ever going to sleep with again. The thought both thrills and terrifies me. I snuggle closer. "Two wanton sex addicts, two chain smokers, denied both their earthly pleasures." Ty groans and the sound excites me much more than it should considering the circumstances. I guess for me, love is an aphrodisiac.

"It's gonna be tough, won't lie," Ty says as I watch the car seats in the center row rock slightly with the rumble of the van. Beth is driving; India's in the passenger seat. We have the two babies with us while Zella and Noah (in separate cars unfortunately) drive everyone else back to the cabin. Not only is it closer than our house, but let's be honest: it's a hell of a lot bigger and nicer than our place. We all agreed that I'd have a better chance at a smooth recovery there. Besides, I've been told that we get to have a second Christmas, another round of Beth's *fabulous* cooking (I'm already preparing for the nausea), and way too many presents.

I got Ty some sex toys, but I guess we'll have to wait to use them. They're wrapped up and shoved underneath our bed, so he's probably already found them and peeled back the tape to peep. Ty can be kind of an ass like that.

"But trust me, babe, we don't need sex or cigs to have a good time." Ty reaches over and gingerly turns my face to look at him. The tenderness in his eyes is enough to melt me into a puddle on the seat, spill me over the edge in a sea of red. "I can write you poems and you can laugh at them. Hell, I'll even buy you some of those trashy, filthy mouthed romance novels you like so much, and you can read them to me. What's that one called where the girl stabs her foster parents with scissors?"

"*Real Ugly?*" I ask with a smile and Ty nods, snapping his fingers.

"That's the one. That shit is wicked fucked, but I'll let you read it to me if it'll make you happy. Oh, and don't forget – you promised we'd read *The Very Hungry Caterpillar* to Noah together. Now *that* book is literary genius."

"I heart the fuck out of you, Ty," I tell him and he nods, like that's simple fact. And you know what? Maybe it is? Maybe my love for Ty is as much a reality, as much a part of the universe as the stars that now twinkle brightly in the sky outside our window?

"I heart the fuck out of you, too, Never Fontaine Nicholas Regali Ross-McCabe." I snort at the ridiculousness of my own name and look into his eyes, searching, wondering if he took our conversation at the hospital seriously. With us, it's always this push and pull, one of us holding the other up when we try to descend into darkness. I won't let what happened to me pull him under. *Hades, you can go fuck yourself. Ty McCabe is mine. Not even the Lord of the Underworld could take him from me.* "And I always will."

7

When we get back to the cabin, Lacey and Trini are waiting for me on the porch. Or maybe they're just watching Zella spin in circles at the edge of the drive, hands on her back and face raised to the sky like she's praying for an intervention. Noah stands close but not too close, hands tucked into the pockets on his pajama pants. I don't see any sign of Tobias Underwood. *Thank God.* For hitting my sister, I hope he gets in an accident and loses his dick to shrapnel.

"Never!" Lacey screams, racing across the gravel towards me. Ty has to step between us to keep her from throwing her arms around me. At this point, I'm still weak from the surgery and the blood loss, and the wounds on my belly feel like I've just been knifed. "Sorry, sorry, sorry," she says as Ty smiles and lets her pass. I rub my hand up and down my right arm, up to my shoulder and down to my elbow. Apparently, the weird pain I felt there when I collapsed was from the internal bleeding, from it irritating the nerves in my arm and shoulder. According to Doctor Pradhan, that was my biggest warning sign, one I felt quite a while before I collapsed on that driveway. "I was so scared you were going to die," Lacey blubbers as we navigate a very weak, very awkward hug. Doesn't matter though. I'm honestly just shocked that a stranger, someone who really has no reason to be here or to care about me, actually gives a shit about whether I live or die. Okay, well Lacey isn't exactly a stranger, but I guess she's my first real female friend in a long time.

"Thank you, Lacey," I say, smiling at Trini as she stays under the porch and tries not to intrude. "I'm glad you're still here and I'm sorry if I ruined your holiday."

"Ruined?" she says, cocking a blonde brow at me. She's in full Barbie form tonight – perfect pink sweater and white jeans, furry black boots, hair coiffed atop her delicate head. Even when we were roommates, it was hard to find Lacey *not* looking perfect. It's kind of a nice constant, a reminder that even though a lot of things have changed lately, my friend is still the same. "Never, don't be stupid," she says, snorting. I roll my eyes as she takes my arm and tries to help me inside. Frankly, I kind of want to go butt into Zella and Noah's conversation, but I'm already tired, halfway asleep.

"I'll keep Little Noah in my room tonight," Beth says as I move inside to the glow of Christmas lights and the soft whisper of carols in the background. There's a black and white movie playing on the big screen, but somebody's muted in. "I don't want anything waking you up," she says as I get ready to tackle the stairs. I want to argue with her, tell her that I'd like, no that I'd *love* to have my son in the room with me tonight. Then I look up at the stairs and a wave of dizziness washes over me. If just thinking about climbing them makes me tired, how can I take care of a baby tonight, too?

I make the smart decision and acquiesce to Beth's demands, curling my hand around the newel post and seriously debating sleeping on the couch tonight.

Ty's right there, of course, dark brows pinched in worry. I watch as he spins his lip ring around, sticks his tongue into the hole. It's one of his coping mechanisms, like running your fingers through your hair or something. I find it absolutely adorable. And the intensity in his eyes? God. It's like he's looking at me for the first time, taking me in, absorbing me. I want to fall into his eyes and drown in their dark depths. I can see him warring between two factions of himself, the part that wants to coddle me and take control, shield me from the world and from myself, and then the other part that knows I'm a whirlwind, a stubborn bitch who won't take *no* for an answer.

"Babe, you want me to carry you up the stairs?" he asks, and I wave him off. I might be injured, but I'm still capable. Ty squeezes his hands into fists and then releases them, nodding briefly. That tender ache in his gaze burns against my skin, and I find myself looking away before I break down in tears again. *He loves me beyond all rational belief.* That much is obvious, so there's no need to cry. Yes, he almost lost me, but I survived. I fucking survived. I am a goddamn survivor.

I reach for the railing and pause as someone appears out of the shadows near the back door. My heart picks up speed and I feel suddenly faint.

Ty and Beth follow my gaze and both freeze, like deer caught in the headlights.

"Hello, Never."

Standing there in an orange sarong and a rusty red tank top is my mother.

8

"The fuck is she doing here?" Ty growls after he and Beth get me tucked into bed. It's so weird for me to be taken care of like this that I find I don't know what to do with myself. My arms and legs feel twitchy, and I want nothing more than to just get up and march down the stairs, ask the bitch myself.

"I … I have no idea," Beth says softly, tugging at her blue flannel sleeping shirt. I know she feels self-conscious when my mom's around sometimes, like she has to look better than her, more professional, put together. That I can totally understand. I think both Beth and me have outgrown the need to have our mother love us – or even really give two fucks that we're alive. Or at least I keep telling myself that; I think I almost believe it. "She said she was at a folk festival." My sister wrinkles up her nose.

"But she's also a lying cunt," I add, sitting up and trying to adjust myself. Ty is there in an instant, helping me, supporting me. And he looks damn good doing it. I'm kind of glad that I'm the girl, that I get to have the babies and he has to stand by. It means he can keep that perfect body of his, that sultry, sexy bad boy look that drove us together in the first place. "And a mooch. And a bitch. Just an all around terrible person."

I look up at Ty, at the hard lines of his jaw, the clenched muscles in his throat as he struggles not to march down those stairs and knock my mother out. He would, too. For me, he'd do anything.

"I'll go talk to her," Beth says, and I immediately feel sorry for her. Having our mother around, in any sort of capacity, is a drain on my sister. Angelica never makes things better, only worse. She arouses those deeply buried hopes in my sisters, the hopes I used to have, that our mom will somehow change overnight, pay attention to them. Since she never does, being around like this is just cruel. "You two rest." Beth pauses to point a finger at Ty and he makes this cute little *you talkin' to me* face that makes my heart flip-flop in my chest. "Ty, I mean you, too. Have you slept at all the last few days?"

I look at Ty, but he quickly glances away, giving my

sister a weak thumbs-up.

"Will do, Mother Dearest," he says before she shakes her head at him and leaves the room. The door closes softly behind her and I'm left to stare at a deranged Santa Claus poster. Noah's mother has some serious decorating issues.

"Ty," I begin as he turns away from me and strips off his shirt. *Dear God.* I feel my voice catch as I stare at the strong hard muscles in his back, the bird tattoos that have so much meaning embedded in each drop of ink that I feel like crying again.

So I only got things with wings. Because I wanted to be free. Every time I got a new tattoo, I promised myself that this was the day I changed everything. This was the day I grew my own wings and flew away.

"Ty." I say his name more forcefully this time, just a split second before he drops his jeans to the floor. I have to look away then. I might be in recovery, but I'm still a sex addict. Still a woman in love.

"What can I do for you, love of my love, heart of my heart?" he asks, flicking off the lights and plunging us both into peaceful darkness. The window is cracked and the soft whisper of cool air teases the cozy warmth of the bedroom, helping to mask some of the shouting I can already hear erupting from downstairs. My mother sure likes to make her presence known.

Ty moves towards me swathed in darkness, stray shafts of moonlight highlighting the piercings on his face. When he gets close enough, I can see *everything.* His mouth shifts into a grin, teeth white in the blue-navy night. Ty crawls in beside me, buck naked, and doesn't act at all ashamed for doing it.

"They say skin to skin contact is helpful in the healing process," he whispers in my ear, managing to find a spot next to me where he can hold me without hurting me. I slide my hand down his thigh and go for the gold, only to have him grab my wrist and press my knuckles against his bare chest.

"Are you really turning down a hand job?" I ask.

"Are you really offering me one right now?" I look at him, try to catch sight of those brown eyes in the dark. "Never, you don't have to worry. No matter what happens, I'll be here. Right here by your fucking side. And I sure as shit ain't taking any favors from you when you're like this. I just want you to rest up and get better, baby. Straight up." I smile but inside, I'm still a little scared. Just a little. But that's normal, right?

"You're such a fucking stud," I say with a sniffle and we both laugh. "Are you sure you won't be grossed out by me? By a baby body and a lot of stretch marks?" I touch my fingers to my belly again and wait in silence for his answer.

"Nev, I've had more sex in the last decade than most people have in their entire lives. I might've been a whore, and an addict, but sex isn't what motivates me. Listen to me, love of my life, the only thing that motivates me is right fucking here." Ty presses his palm to my chest and I feel my heartbeat pick up, slamming against my rib cage, so loud I'm sure even Beth and my mom can hear it downstairs. Before I can question him any further, ask him if he really stayed awake for the last three days, I hear the soft whisper of his breath against my ear, and I have my answer.

9

I manage to make it two full days without seeing my mom. One might think she'd be interested in visiting her daughter, a daughter she drove away for five years, a daughter who recently lost her baby. But no. No. My mother uses Noah's cabin as a hotel, so she can go to and from her folk festival without having to pay for a room. Apparently, this stupid event of hers is being held at a farm not too far from us. Honestly, I doubt that 'festival' is even an appropriate word for the event. My mom spends a lot of time hanging out and fucking random people, smoking pot, dancing. For all I know, it might just be a group of middle-aged dudes in a trailer, parked on a shady corner of some fallow corn field.

Well, two days in, and I finally get up enough strength to go downstairs and sit in the living room. Ty, the devilish little sweet that he is, props my feet up in his lap and actually gives me a foot massage – a really, *really* good one.

"You're a god," I whisper and Ty flashes me a naughty grin.

"Remember that when we're allowed to have sex again." I roll my eyes and shake my head, a smile curling my lips. It's hard to stay mad when the air smells like pine, when your little sisters are gathered around the Christmas tree, waiting to give you a second chance at the holiday you might've missed forever. Of course, that's before I get a whiff of Beth's cooking and my stomach turns over twice before I manage to get ahold of myself.

"Look at you." My mother's voice is unmistakable as she saunters into the room in a tinkling of bells. I bet she thinks she looks real pretty in her big gypsy skirt and her hip scarf. The fresh, sharp scent of weed follows her in, making me twice as queasy as I was before. "You must feel like a queen."

Ty's hands go still, too still, and I worry that this situation is going to escalate out of control before I can stop it. I give him a look which he returns, and try to tell him with my eyes that she isn't worth it. I mean, we both know that, but if my mom is good at anything, it's inciting feelings of frustration in those around her.

"Nice to see you, too, Angelica," I say, trying to keep my voice calm. My little siblings, especially Darla, watch the interaction between us carefully. My heart already aches for her, knowing that one day, she'll realize what I do: Angelica doesn't care about anyone but herself. It takes me a moment to collect myself, to bite back the angry words I want to say. *How can you be so selfish? How can you care so little?*

"So, can I hold my grandson now or what?" My mom pauses in the center of the room, her head silhouetted in the middle of the oversized TV screen, like some sort of inside joke between me and the universe. *See, look at that. In this movie, the mom actually gives a rat's ass about her children. How weird is that?*

"That depends on your answer," I whisper, my voice lower and harsher than I intend. *I cut her off. I did. She's a cancer. Our relationship, it can't be saved.* I look at Ty again, at the ruby rings on his fingers, the ones that match the piercings in his face. I love how he fucking puts himself together like that. I won't tell him this, but he kind of looks like a pirate right now and I love it. "You told Beth I needed to learn a lesson. What the fuck does that mean?"

"Language," Beth chirps, her motherly attitude only slightly subdued by Angelica's presence.

"I didn't say you *needed* to learn one. I said you just might. And I did say I was sorry. Miscarriages aren't exactly fun." I purse my lips so tight, I feel like my mouth just might fall off my face. I almost hope it does, that blood sprays everywhere, right into Angelica's eyes.

And then I hope it blinds her.

"What are you even doing here?" I whisper, not even bothering to correct her, to tell her that I almost died, or that I'm still pregnant. Hell, it's not like she cares either way. If I had bled out, left this world for the next, would she have even cried? Or maybe she'd have been too busy at some 'folk festival' to come to my funeral. "You couldn't be bothered to make it to the hospital."

"Oh come off it, Never," she says, leaning down in a swirl of skirts and the lingering scent of nag champa. The smell of her, of her weed and her cigarettes and her incense, it used to comfort me. Now all it does is make my stomach turn. "The world doesn't revolve around you and your problems."

"How much jail time would I get if I punched this bitch out?" Ty asks, almost conversationally. Angelica scowls at him, brushing some copper curls behind her ear as she stands up and crosses her arms over her chest. Normally, when the shit gets going, so does Angelica. If she's still here then it means she must have nowhere else to go. And no money. No worries, though. As soon as she steals enough from my sisters or begs some off Beth, she'll leave. "And keep your hands off our son, lady. You got that?"

"Based on what I've heard about you, are you sure you have the right to be so choosy?"

"What the fuck is that supposed to mean?" Ty asks quietly, putting my feet aside and standing up. His fists are clenched by his sides and his arm muscles are tense beneath the layer of brightly colored tattoos that sweep up to his shoulders.

Movement in the corner of the room catches my eye,

and I look to find Jade squeezing into the rec room in the back like she's fleeing the scene of a crime. And then I remember that Ty told Jade all sorts of things about himself in his attempt to help her, things she probably relayed right back to my mother.

Things could get ugly in here real quick. I mean, I don't really think Ty would ever hit my mother or anything, but I also don't want things said that can't be unsaid. Insults and slights are the food of dark demons, and Ty and I are just starting to starve ours out of existence.

"It means a dirty little prostitute like yourself doesn't really have room to talk."

Holy. Fucking. Shit.

But of course my mother isn't done spreading evil in her wake, infecting the earth like fallout from a nuclear bomb.

"How much is it anyway if I want some?" When she literally reaches out towards Ty's crotch like she's going to grab him right in front of my little sisters, I almost completely lose it. Okay, so I actually *really* lose it. I don't see the world, blinded for a few seconds there by red hot color that swirls in my eyes like a swarm of angry bees. Before I even realize it, I'm up and off the couch, shoving my mother back before Ty can grab a hold of me.

"I just lost my *baby*," I scream at her, not caring that my family's watching anymore. "I almost fucking died! And all you can think to do is come here and try to demean the one person in this world that makes me feel like I'm lucky to be alive? You go to hell!" I screech, fighting against Ty's gentle hold on me, keeping me back from doing what I really want to do. I want to hit my mom so hard that her face hurts just a fraction of how bad my heart does. "Get out of here and never come back! I don't ever want to see you again."

I break down in sobs then, not because I'm weak, but because I'm strong. I'm stronger than this, better than this. Tears are not a sign of weakness, just a reminder that life happens. There's nothing wrong with feeling the pain as it hits you, letting it wash over and through you. I should know; I spent years fighting it off in all the wrong ways. If I'd just let it come, if I'd only let it come.

"You are so overdramatic, Never," my mom huffs, her long purple pendant earrings swaying as she turns away. I collapse into Ty and turn my face to his chest, breathing in his scent to block out hers. He smells like ... like butterflies and love and cloves and laundry detergent. His hand, when it touches the back of my head, is unbelievably tender.

"You have about five minutes to grab your stuff and go," Ty whispers over the top of my head. I can't see his face, but I bet I know what it looks like. Ty is strong and beautiful and so imperfect that he's perfect.

"And you're going to enforce that how?" Angelica asks. I can't look at her right now, so I bury my face in my husband's chest and I let the tears flow free. I'm upset. I'm still upset. Yeah, I'm getting through this, but it's not like I'm a superhero, like I can put on a cape and wipe away the problems of the world. "I've had plenty of men hit me before, so go ahead, give me your best shot."

Ty stays right where he is, holding me, supporting me like I've never had anyone support me before.

"Wouldn't give you the satisfaction if you begged

me," Ty says, raising his hand to stroke my hair back. I pull away from him just enough so that I can breathe, my eyes focused on the wet stain my tears have left on his hot pink T-shirt. It says, *Real Men Give Feminist Rants* on the front. It's one of my favorite designs, save for the little skeleton fetus shirt that Ty gave me. I wonder if I'll be able to wear it now, considering everything that happened. I still have a baby inside of me, but it's hard knowing there were two babies, twins. Ectopic pregnancies aren't viable at all, meaning that one baby was doomed from the start. Why is life so cruel? There was no choice there, no chance, just the ringing of doom from the moment of conception. That makes me sad, really sad.

"Who the hell are you anyway? You're not a part of this family, just some freeloader. Never, sweetie, trust me on this one. Guys like this, they don't hang around long after the fun is over and the money's run dry."

I turn around then and look her in her hazel eyes, the ones that are so like mine I could scream. I wish I didn't have any part of her inside of me, not a single scrap of DNA, not a single good memory. If I could, I would just erase it all, like I did with my name. Never Fontaine Regali became Never Nicholas Ross, and it felt good. Too good. Perfect.

"I want you to go," I whisper, afraid that my voice will fail me. She ignores me, of course, and moves into the kitchen in a sway of skirts, like nothing at all has happened between us. I listen to the sound of clinking glass and know that even if I can't see her, she's pouring herself a drink. All around us, the room remains silent, my sisters' faces focused on me, waiting, wondering.

Once again, I force myself to be the bigger person in the situation and plaster a smile on my face.

"Is it almost time for presents?" I ask, moving away from Ty and feeling that sudden coldness, that achingly palpable sense of his absence. Even though I feel like shit, like my belly is tight and my insides are all scrambled up, I walk over to India and sit down, reaching out my arms for my son.

When I hug him tight to my chest, I look up and meet Ty's eyes, see the softening around the edges. He must know what I'm just starting to realize: you don't have to have a good mom to know how to be one. Even though she doesn't love me, it doesn't matter, because I'll love my son enough to make up for all of it.

10

I sit outside by the pond, curled up on a wooden Adirondack chair, and watch snowflakes kiss the water's glossy black surface. It's dark enough now that I can't see the opposite shore, giving the impression that the pond stretches on for forever, delves even deeper into the infinite mystery of the unknown. It's as cold as my mother's heart out here, but only half as empty. I fight back the chill trying to work its way into my bones by running my fingers across the face of the photo album Beth gave me as a Christmas present.

I feel the ghost of a smile kiss my lips as I flip open the cover and examine my father's face, a face I have not seen in so long that I'd forgotten what it looked like. And I feel bad for that, I do.

"Papa, why do butterflies have such pretty wings?"

"Because, sweet thing, my little Never say Never, they don't just want to fly; they want to soar."

"How ya feelin', babe?" Ty asks from his spot in the grass. He's laying on his back and looking up at the stars with an intensity that would make me blush if I were them. As if in response, I feel like some of the diamonds twinkle, just for him.

I look down at Ty, clutching a cigarette tight in his ringed fingers. It's our last one, literally. Ty went through all of our stuff and tossed the rest out. Neither of us missed the memo about how smoking can quadruple your risk of having an ectopic pregnancy. Normally, I'm not so quick to jump on the anti-smoking bandwagon, but I still feel like I was kicked repeatedly in the stomach by Fezzik from *The Princess Bride.*

"A little bit of good, a little bit of bad," I admit, shrugging my shoulders and turning the pages in the album. The trauma of losing my father the way I did, of watching his murderer walk free, of seeing my mother's blank and bored face when she found us in the living room, it had all royally fucked up my memories. I hadn't remembered his hair so dark, his eyes so bright. "I guess it all equals out to a sort of numbness."

"Ah, kitten, no." Ty sits up with a clenching of stomach muscles that makes my entire body flush from head to toe. Six weeks of no sex, huh? I've barely lasted four days. "Don't go back to that place. Don't let *her* shove you back into that hole."

"Did you seriously just call me kitten?" I ask and Ty grins, flashing me a dimpled smile. His mood improved ridiculously fast after our dog threw up on my mom's expensive hemp purse. Oh, and Noah's dog bit her and stole the organic wheat muffin she was eating. All in all, the day played out as I'd expected, but it wasn't all bad.

"You mewl like one when we're in bed together, so I thought it was fitting." I smack Ty on the top of his dark head with the album and then plop it back into my lap, carefully avoiding the soreness in my lower belly. "Mind if I take a look see with ya?"

"If you keep talking like that, I'll send you back inside and you can drink kombucha with Angelica." Ty wrinkles his nose and scoots close to me, resting his head on my arm as I pause on a picture of my dad with Beth, Zella, Jade, and me. We're standing in front of him with big grins on our faces, hands clasped together, copper hair shimmering in the sun. My dad has this sloppy smile on, half hidden by his goatee. His shoulder length hair is shaggy and unkempt, but he has this rugged handsomeness to him that I can see reflected in the promise of my baby's chubby face.

"Can I poison her cum-what's-it-called instead?" Ty wrinkles up his beautiful face as I look over at him with a raised brow.

"Kombucha. It's basically rotten tea with sugar," I say with a shrug of my shoulders. Me, I'd rather have good old sweet tea any day. I wonder briefly why my mom was always so up in arms about me having moved to California. Honestly, she probably would've fit in much better there than in Mississippi.

"Well, whatever it's called, I hope she chokes on it. Never," Ty says, getting serious all of a sudden, "I know how hard it is to have a fucked up mom. You know that. And unfortunately for you, yours is still around to keep fucking up, but we've made it through way worse than this shit. I guess what I'm trying to say is: feel everything. Feel it, let it hurt, and then slap a Band-Aid on it. And if that Band-Aid just so happens to be my naked body inside of yours, all the better."

"Only five and a half weeks to go!" I say with false enthusiasm. Ty sits up and gets on his knees so that our faces are level. Even in the dark, he's beautiful. No, no, *especially* in the dark he's beautiful. His face is chiseled from starlight and his hair is one with the night. I literally pinch myself to make sure I'm not dreaming him up.

"Until then, we'll find other ways to entertain ourselves," he says, leaning forward to kiss me. Our lips meet in a rush of heat broken only by the tiny snowflakes that fall, punctuating all of that warmth with little bits of cold. Ty doesn't use his tongue, just the force of his mouth against mine, a slight pressure that builds up so quickly I feel like I'm falling over the edge.

A voice being cleared behind us draws us both up and out of the spell that's been cast, wrapping both Ty and me in a web of tortured beauty that leaves me breathless.

When I tear my gaze from my husband's smirk and glance over my shoulder, I see Zella waiting. She's wearing a white cable-knit sweater and has a quilt thrown over one arm.

"Is it okay if I talk to you for a minute?" she asks, her voice quivering with a thousand fears I wish I could've protected her from. It's too late to go back on all of that now, but I know I have to help my sister find the right path, before she stumbles down a million twisted crossroads like I did.

"Sure thing, sis," Ty says with a wink, rising to his black booted feet and looking down at me. He touches the side of my face affectionately before moving away, walking backwards towards the warm lights of the cabin. "Don't stay out here too long or I'll miss you so much it fucking hurts." Ty presses his palm to his lips and then tosses me a kiss.

I'm smiling when Zella comes over and sits beside me. I make sure to clear her a space, snuggling up to my sister like I haven't done in years.

"Pictures of dad, huh? I can't tell if Beth was being cruel or what." Zella touches the page with her fingers, fingers that are so similar to mine that it's almost eerie. "Why would she give this to you now, after everything?"

"Because she wants me to remember," I say, tilting my head to the side. "For years I've blocked these memories." I pause and bite my lip. "And for years I blamed him instead of her, for leaving all the time, for not standing up to her more, even for dying." Tears try desperately to claw their way out and at first, I think I'm succeeding. But then, just like the snowflakes hitting the surface of the lake, drops of liquid hit the page with a silence that seems suddenly loud. Raucous, earsplitting silence. Now I know I'm starting to lose it.

Zella takes my hand under the blanket and warms my chilled fingers with her own.

"I'm sorry for what I did, Never. Or rather, what I *didn't* do. If I had said something, stood up for you against Mom and Beth and ... " Zella wrinkles her nose. "*Jade,* then would you have stayed?"

I don't know the answer to that question, so I just shake my head.

"Do you think you could ever forgive me?" she asks instead.

"Zella, I forgave you a long time ago."

"Not just for what happened with Mom and Luis, but for all the things I said on the driveway, for being so petty and cruel and self-centered when you needed me most. And for ... for Noah." Her voice comes out in a whisper, as soft and unique as the snowflake that alights on her lips as she turns to look at me. My sister's hazel eyes find mine, like a mimicry of the cold gray night that surrounds us.

"If I've learned anything from being with Ty," I say, feeling my lips twitch into a soft smile. See, just his name is enough to get me, to wrap around my heart and hold it tight in the world's most perfect embrace. "It's that honesty is one of the most important things there is. Without it, we might as well be living in a virtual reality, some sideways universe of our own making. Well, I spent enough years there and I don't want to be there anymore. You said what you needed to say, Zella, and I don't hold any of it against you." She takes a deep breath, but I'm not done. "What I do hold against you, however, is the fact that you and Noah don't seem to be doing so well. What the hell is up with that?"

"We ... I ... we had sex in the pond," she whispers, her entire body going slack like the weight of her confession weighs as much as the whole world. "When Tobias was here, the night before you collapsed."

I glance over at the water with a raised brow. And I thought Ty and I were kinky. Huh.

"But with everything that happened, I haven't had a chance to process it. I mean, Tobias and I broke up *again,* and I don't know what's happening with school and Beth won't talk about it with me right now – "

I cut her off by laying my head against her shoulder.

"Stop processing, Zella, and start living."

My little sister sighs, but even she has nothing to say against that.

11

I head inside, leaving Zella alone with the album. Even if she doesn't realize it, she has some healing to do, too. Otherwise, she never would've ended up with a douche like Tobias Underwood. I try to sympathize with the guy, try to remind myself that my sister hit him just as many times as he hit her, but I don't care. I still hate the stupid fuck.

Anyway, pain is relative. Zella might not have

suffered through the same things as I have, but she could still be hurting just as much.

I glance over my shoulder with a small smile, crunching across the frozen grass in my new black slippers. Lacey and Trini got me these, excited to show me their matching yellow and pink pairs respectively. *Now we're shoe triplets!* Pretty sure that's what she said to me. My mouth twitches a little and even though my stomach is killing me, swearing up and down that I must've done a thousand crunches or something, I smile a little, just a little.

Feels good. I think I'd like to keep doing it.

When I step inside, I find Ty sleeping on the couch with our son on his chest.

I stop like I've been frozen in place, tears pricking my eyes, my heart thudding painfully in my chest.

This might be the most beautiful sight I've ever seen – Ty with his hair wet from a shower, mussy and cute as hell, shirtless, and our son, fast asleep with an armful of rings and bracelets wrapped around him. It does not escape my notice that Little Noah is dressed in a Dracula costume, complete with cape.

I clamp my hands over my mouth and just stare. I could look at the two of them until my eyes rotted out of my head and I'd never miss my sight, not with this image burned into my brain.

"It won't last," my mother says softly, appearing in the flickering light from the kitchen's fireplace. She has a blue glass tumbler in one hand and a cigarette clutched in the other. I know Noah doesn't like anyone smoking in the cabin, know he's told her that. And I'm sure that even though *I* didn't say anything about the ectopic pregnancy and the cigarette smoke and all that, that Beth probably has. Add onto that the fact that my son is in the room, and I just can't help the scowl that twists my mouth.

I drop my hands to my sides and fight against the surge of anger I feel towards Angelica. It doesn't help, never has helped.

"It will last," I assure her, stepping all the way inside the cabin and closing the French door behind me. "Ty McCabe is my soul mate."

My mother laughs, but I don't care. Her bitterness is all the punishment I could ever wish for. It hurts to hate yourself that much. Trust me, I know. I've been there.

"Are you going to run from me forever? I mean, you're living at the house now. We can't exactly avoid each other, now can we?"

I shrug.

"You're never around. It's honestly not that hard to forget you even exist."

I move around the sectional sofa and pause, gazing down at my lover and my vampire clad child with a smile. When I reach over and move Ty's arm, his red and green Christmas bracelets jingle like bells and Noah coos. I lift my son into my arms with a small grunt of pain. Any movement that causes me to use my abs – which is actually pretty much fucking everything if you think about it – hurts. But I don't care. I'll hurt for my son, my Ty, my family.

"Are you ever going to let me hold him?" she asks, her voice a little more gentle, a little less cynical. I know it's all a front, have known it for years, but I can't stop myself from feeling for her. *Fuck.* I grit my teeth and turn around.

"Maybe if you put out your fucking cigarette?" It comes out as a question, and I can't help myself, looking down at Ty to see if he's awake. He's not. I look back at my mother, watch as she drops her cig into the kitchen sink and leaves it there for someone else to clean up. *Hypocrite.* She never let any of us smoke in her house, but I guess it doesn't matter if it's someone else's.

She's wearing a bra today, which is a miracle, and a white tank with her loud yellow and blue striped skirt. Even though the outfit's a little weird, she's still pretty in it. That both bothers and excites me. I'm happy to know our strong Southern genes keep us youthful, but I also kind of wish that my mom's outside looked as bleak as her inside.

When she holds out her arms for my son, I have to take a serious breath, think really hard about what I'm doing. I decide that it's time, that I should do this not for her, but for me.

"Finally," she says, and I just close my eyes against the anger. *You'll get none of that from me right now.* "Even with a mongrel for a daddy, you're kind of cute." I snap my eyes open and start to speak when I see my mother nuzzling my son's face. He smiles at her, doesn't even cry. I wonder if it's because she's wearing a bracelet of bells around her wrist. They jingle as she rocks him, like his papa's bracelets do.

I bite my lower lip against tears. I suddenly want to say all of the things I'm thinking, tell her everything, give her another chance to apologize for Luis. But I can't. I can't because I know without even asking that she'll disappoint me.

"But we all know that dads don't matter so much, right? I mean, look at your sisters. They all have deadbeat fathers and they still turned out okay."

I swallow hard.

"You say my sisters, but what about *my* dad?"

My mom says nothing, just spins in a slow lazy circle with my son in her arms. The glow of the Christmas tree makes her copper hair gleam like a fresh new penny in a beam of sunlight.

"You didn't seem to care when he died, so ... was he a deadbeat, too?"

My mother pauses in her rocking to look right at me. I see the hint of a truth lingering in her eyes, like the tip of an iceberg buoyed on the salty sea.

"Why did he die, Mom? Was it a custody thing? Were you going to take Jade from him?"

Angelica says nothing, instead deciding she's had enough of her grandson. She hands him back to me and shakes out her arms, like being nice for twenty seconds was too much for her.

"You were young, Never. You don't know what you saw. Besides, why would Luis care about Jade anyway? Even if your father wanted her, Luis didn't."

"I know what I saw," I whisper back, but Angelica is already leaving, heading back into the kitchen for another drink. "Luis killed my father."

"He had no motive," my mother quips, glancing over her shoulder at me. "All he cared about then was fucking me and drinking away my money."

When she disappears around the corner, I close my eyes and hug my baby close. When I open them and look back at Ty, I find him sitting up and staring at me with a longing ache in his eyes, drinking me in like I matter.

I matter.

And that's all I give a wild shit about.

12

New Year's Eve and my mom is still at the cabin. Fortunately, she avoids Ty and me like the plague, but that hasn't stopped her from throwing barbs at everyone else. I even heard her give Beth crap over her haircut, like my sister isn't busy enough taking care of a half-dozen kids, most of which aren't even hers. I try not to engage, but it's like walking through a swarm of stinging bees and not swatting at each and every one of them.

"Too bad I won't get any champagne tonight," I say, resting my chin on my arms and staring at the bottles that Noah produces from a paper grocery bag. "No booze, no cigarettes, just a bellyful of baby, McCabe baby at that. He makes ornery little fuckers, if you didn't already know that."

Noah smiles and moves over to the freezer, opening it and peering inside.

"No booze, but there are strawberries. Ty asked me to get some when I was at the store. Did you want a smoothie or something?" I smile as I put my hand on my belly. Not only did Ty remember my addiction, but I also find Noah adorable, even if he's not my tortured other half. He seriously needs to be a part of this family, one way or another. Besides, I can see it in both their eyes: my sister and Noah Scott are hopelessly, tragically, inextricably in love with each other.

"I would love that, Noah, thanks."

He proceeds to get out the smoothie ingredients while I watch and wait, deciding exactly how I should bring up the subject of him and Zella.

I decide to start with this.

"So I hear you banged my sister in the pond."

Noah drops the bag of frozen strawberries and it explodes, sending bright red fireworks across the floor. He immediately drops to his knees and starts to pick them up, glancing over at me from beneath a fall of liquid gold hair. When I try to rise to my feet to help, I feel rough, warm hands close over my shoulders.

"I've got it, babe."

Ty kneels next to Noah and doesn't even pretend he didn't hear what I just said.

"You banged my sister-in-law, huh?"

Noah grunts but doesn't bother to elaborate. If I'm not mistaken, a red flush colors his cheeks, bright enough to rival the round crimson spots of strawberry littered across the floor. Ty chooses not to take the hint and continues to prod at my high school sweetheart.

"And in the pond? Must've been cold as dick out there. How'd you ever manage that one?"

"It just happened," Noah whispers, pushing the half full bag in front of him as he moves across the floor. He pauses for a moment and adjusts the shirt that Ty got him for Christmas. Yes, that's right. Not only did the love of my life name our kid after my ex, he also bought him a present. The shirt is tight and fits in all the right places. Don't get the wrong idea here, I only noticed because Zella did. She hasn't been able to take her eyes off of him. "I'm in love with her, but she ... " He trails off and stares down at the T-shirt like he's trying to memorize the design. The pixelated white knight stares up at him, sword raised, his blonde hair shining under a printed sun. *Nice guys finish last, but usually, they get the highest score.*

My husband certainly has a thing for tees with catch phrases on them.

"She thinks I'm still in love with you," Noah says, not looking at Ty or me or anyone else.

"No," I tell him, drawing his blue eyes up to mine. "She's too afraid to find out what it feels like to have love, real, true, honest to God, shatter the heart and tantalize the spirit kind of love. It's a disease in our family, and only you can be the cure."

Ty chuckles, and I smile, but we don't get to revel in

this feeling of friendship that's blossoming between the three of us because, of course, my mom won't let things be easy or right or perfect.

"I found this," she says, storming into the kitchen and lifting up the photo album that Beth gave me. Her fingers are curled around the spine like she wishes she could choke the life out of those photographs the same way Luis choked the life out of my Papa. If the bitch had stuck around long enough to participate in any family time, she would've already seen it. "What the fuck is this?"

I stand up off of the stool because I don't like the tone of her voice, the insinuation in her eyes, like this album has *anything* at all to do with her. Inside, I've always been a mess. On the outside, I can handle my shit. I've fought off more unwanted advances than I can remember, told off more people that I care to count, and defended myself against the worst of words – many of which were true. Even if I'm hurting and my stomach aches and I wish my mother would spontaneously combust, I can still stand up to her. I did it before and it cost me everything. This, this is nothing.

"If I didn't know any better," I begin as Ty and Noah rise to their feet behind me, "I'd think you *wanted* to find a reason to hate me. You're cruel, Angelica, and you're lazy. Oh, and you're the most self-centered person I've ever met in my life. But you left my room locked and frozen in time for five years, so tell me, what is your problem? I can't figure you out."

My mother turns her head, just enough that her curls tumble over her shoulders and her earrings, a pair of bright blue butterflies, swing with the motion.

And then she throws my father into the flames of the fireplace.

A scream rips from my throat, a tearing sound that twists my heart in two. My dad is already dead, already an enigma, a mystery, a collection of forgotten memories, and now these few, few pictures, this symbol of love from my sister, is burning like the hatred in my mother's eyes.

I rush forward before I can stop myself, but a hand wraps around my waist, pulling me back. Before I even realize what he's doing, Ty McCabe is reaching into the fire and ripping the album out of the orange and yellow, the flickering biting mouth of the fire.

He drops it on the stones in front of the fireplace and shakes out his fingers, cursing as he steps on the book with his black combat boots. Within seconds, the book is smoldering but no longer in flames, crisped at the edges but still intact.

My mother doesn't even say a damn a word, just turns and flees like the coward she is while I rush to Ty McCabe, my soul mate, my one in seven billion, and take his hand in mine. His rough fingers curl around mine while I try to assess the damage. A few pink spots dot his knuckles, like the wings of Ty's monarch butterfly tattoo are fading into his skin, stealing away its flight.

I look up into his brown eyes and even though what he did was a stupid, stupid, stupid thing to do, I heart the fuck out of him for it.

"We need to get something on these burns," I say as he traps me in a hug with his right hand and pulls us together, firmly but not roughly, ever aware of the still healing scars on my belly.

"Never," he says as I try to pull away, to take care of him the way he's always taking care of me. Ty won't let, keeping me close, leaning down and finding my lips, tasting them softly. "I want you to look at me, and I want you to let it all fall away."

"Ty, I – " He squeezes me a little tighter, just enough, his face so soft and tender and beautiful that I can barely breathe.

"Just let it go, baby. Take a breath and say goodbye to the bullshit."

I can feel the frustration and the panic and the … *rage.* I feel so much rage right now, I can barely stand straight. My last memories of my father niggle at the edges of my brain, bringing up several thoughts that I've long since kept buried but never forgot. *Why* did Luis kill my dad? I'd wondered before if it was about custody (even if Angelica denies it), but then, Luis didn't try to make a reappearance in our lives until much, much later. So why? Why?

"He had no motive," my mother quips, glancing over her shoulder at me. "All he cared about then was fucking me and drinking away my money."

My breath catches sharply.

Because my mother asked him to.

The revelation rocks me to my core, like the big Pacific Coast quake everyone's always worrying about. Luis is a lazy drunk, a drifter, a useless sack of nothing. Of *course* he wouldn't have come up with the idea to kill my father on his own. It seems so obvious now, but …

Besides, why would Luis care about Jade anyway? Even if your father wanted her, Luis didn't.

Angelica's words from last night flood my brain until

it's impossible for me to form a single, rational thought.

I take a shuddering breath and try to wriggle away from Ty, but he's not budging.

Noah, on the other hand, looks like he's just snapped in half. Both Ty and I watch in bewildered fascination as the blonde haired, blue-eyed boy from my past whirls out of the kitchen like a demon wrenched from the depths of hell.

I'm almost as shocked by his actions as I am by my epiphany.

"I want you out," he says, voice low and simmering with an anger that could've only built after years and years and years of my mother's bullshit. It's so ... deep. Angelica is the one who tore us apart, who broke Jade, who twisted Zella, who enslaved Beth. And Noah's had a front row seat to it all.

"Excuse me, young man?" Angelica asks, her voice still perfectly portraying the damaged victim. Or maybe she's just shocked because Noah has always been so damn nice to her.

"I want you off my property immediately. Pack your things and go."

Ty finally lets me go, our fingers curling together as I pull him towards the living room to see the confrontation taking place. He cringes a little when I touch his burned hand, but he doesn't stop, pausing behind me in the kitchen entrance.

Beth is standing behind one of the couches with Darla's little fingers curled in her hand. Lettie and Lorri sit on the couch next to India, a book clutched in her frozen hands. Everyone looks confused, surprised, maybe even a little bit nervous, but nobody looks as bad as Jade.

She stares at our mother with quivering lips and tears streaking her dark makeup down her face. Something else happened before my mother brought that album to me, something terrible. I can see it in my sister's face.

"Noah, what's going on?" Zella asks, taking a tentative step forward. The lights in the living room, the glow from the second fireplace, all of it presses this warm cozy aura down around us that's so at odds with the emotions in the room that I could scream.

"I want Angelica out. Now. Take your things and go. I've seen so much abuse from you and I've never said a word, but I'm saying one now. I can't *fucking* take it anymore. You ... you're awful and you're wicked. I won't sit back and watch it anymore."

"Well, you can forget about showing your face on my property ever again," my mother snaps, thrusting a hand out at Noah. The colored bangles on her arm ring, the sound a strange, terrible mimicry of the beauty that Ty's jewelry makes.

Without another word, she turns on her heel and disappears up the steps to her guest room.

I consider following after her, blurting the words from my lips that I've only just figured out.

You asked Luis to kill Dad. You. You. You. Deny it all you want, I can finally see it now.

I lick my lips, heart fluttering wildly in my throat, and then glance back at McCabe. He's starting at and through me, and I know he can tell I've come to sort some sort of conclusion. Then I catch sight of his injured hand, fingers curled, a slight quiver in his arm that he's trying to fight back. Going after my mom, yelling at her, confronting her, it won't do any good. I should know that by now.

In that instant I have to make a decision: choose the past or the present, the rage or the love, my mother or Ty.

I choose Ty.

I'd choose Ty a billion times over.

I step towards him, taking his left hand in my own, careful not to touch his burns.

"There's some aloe vera in the kitchen," I say, fighting back tears, frustration, knowing that none of it matters. *My husband reached through flames for me.*

"What are you even doing? Trying to be a hero?" Zella asks, and I glance over in time to see Noah cringe. I have no idea what she's so angry about, but I don't have the energy to deal with her right now. "Just butt out, Noah. This is family business." She darts up the stairs and disappears into her own room, slamming the door behind her.

A few seconds later, Lacey and Trini appear, each carrying one of the babies who, as if they can sense the atmosphere, both decide to start crying. In the strange chaos that ensues, it's hard to keep track of everybody and everything that's going on.

A few minutes after we hear my mom's station wagon pull down the driveway, Beth comes sprinting into the kitchen with sweat dripping down her face, her eyes wide and pupils dilated.

"Has anyone seen Darla?"

13

Beth is sobbing so hard that she can barely move her lips, can barely tell the dispatcher on the other end of the line what the problem is. At least Lorri spied Angelica from the window by the front door, putting Darla in the backseat. At least we know she isn't in the pond or in the forest or something as equally horrific as that. Doesn't seem to be helping Beth much though.

I stand beside her, my son in my arms, my eyes on

the album that lies by my sister's elbow. Some of the pictures are a little warped on the edges, but for the most part, the smiles and the memories of my father remain. As soon as I get a chance, I'm going to scan them in and upload them to the cloud. As of right now, I have to watch as Ty gently untangles the phone from Beth's fingers.

Just as I'd feared, just as my mother had known, the police can't do anything. Beth might be Darla's mother for all intents and purposes, but legally, she has no claim on her. They're simply sisters, and Angelica is technically her mom. Technically. As in, the same way a guy that donates sperm at the sperm bank is a father to his long forgotten seed.

It's a stretch.

"I can't believe this is happening," my sister says, her crestfallen face splotchy and tear stained. "Darla is ... Mom left the day Darla came home from the hospital and didn't come back for six weeks. I fed her, changed her diapers. I made every doctor's appointment. I even *named* her. Did Mom tell you that?" she spins to look at me, hazel eyes piercing. I swear, the gold flecks in them glimmer with barely suppressed rage. "She told me to choose and I did. And now she wants to take *my* daughter and run off without answering her fucking PHONE!" Beth stands up and slams her palms on the counter, making Mini McCabe cry. Without a second's hesitation, my sister reaches out and takes my son from me, calming him down with a practiced hand and hugging him to her chest like a lifeline.

I cross my arms over my chest and watch her, my heart breaking all over again.

Angelica only took Darla to prove a point, to stab a needle into the family unit and watch it bleed. She doesn't give two shits about her own child.

"What if she takes her to one of her awful friends' houses?" Beth asks, referencing a lifetime of 'sleepovers' that we were forced to endure. I remember once when my mom took Beth and me to some nudist party thing and made us sit in the corner while she smoked pot and had sex with some random guy. Beth was seven; I was five. "I can't even believe this is happening. I can't ... I don't even know how to process this."

"We could drive back to the house and see if she went home?" Zella asks, looking over at Noah. Something strange passes between them, and I can only wonder what happened after Noah went after her. Because he did. That's right. He actually went up the stairs and used a skeleton key to force his way into her room. For once in his life, Noah looks like he's actually ready to fight for something. There's still tension between them, but since Zella's down here and not in hiding, they must've worked at least a few of their issues out. I see them exchange a glance, but can't summon up the energy to smile. Angelica's actions are overshadowing everything, including the fact that the new year is less than minutes away.

Beth nods sharply and hands Mini McCabe back to Ty. I watch as my lover takes our child in one bandaged hand and one ringed one, supporting him with a jingle of bracelets as we exchange a look of our own.

"Go. But be careful. The roads are icy and there are always lots of drunk people on these country roads." Beth pauses. "Not to mention the fact that it's New

Year's fucking Eve." Another pause as she puts her hands on her hips and spins in a slow circle. "You know what? Maybe you shouldn't go. I don't want to put you in danger, too."

"It's not a big deal, Beth, we'll be careful." Zella takes a step closer to her and then stops. There's an awkwardness between them, born of Zella's expulsion from school and her subsequent lie. Yet another issue this family will have to deal with together. If I have to, I'll bring it up myself. I've seen what happens when someone runs from conflict; I've *lived* it. "You're not going to sleep or eat or even sit still until we find Darla. Let Noah and me go, and we can at least rule out one place she might be. Do you have Mom's new boyfriend's phone number?"

"I don't even know his name," Beth whispers, reaching down to touch the singed album. Her eyes alight with tears again and she shakes her head before another sob breaks from her throat. "Please let her be okay. Please, please, please."

I leave the room and Ty follows, moving up to stand beside me. I can't keep myself from looking at his bandaged hand.

"I fucking love your face," I tell him and he nods, like this is simple fact.

"I heart the freaking shit out of yours," he confirms, and I manage a slight smile. I haven't had a chance to talk to Ty about my seemingly obvious revelation. *Mom wanted Dad dead. Period.* How, why, I had never really made this connection before is just a sign of how damaged I am. It seems so obvious now. I mean, it's the only real explanation there is. Luis was a piece of shit, but why would he decide to hit our home, kill my father, all for no reason at all? The only connection here is Angelica. The only question left is *why*.

"You shouldn't have done what you did, but I'm thankful for it."

Ty steps in close, cocooning our little McCabe family unit in a tight warmth that makes my heart swell at the same moment it cracks for Beth. For Darla.

"I'd do anything for you, Never Ross. I told you that before, that I'd wade through knee-deep shit for you? Well, I meant the fuck out of that. I want you to remember that." He kisses my forehead and I sigh. "What now?"

"I think I need to find Jade," I tell him and he nods, lips pursed. We're both scared for Jade, both see signs of the same darkness that taints our own souls. I put my hand on his hard bicep and squeeze, enjoying the strength of the muscles beneath his inked flesh. "If I'm not back in twenty minutes, come looking for me." I'm only half joking; Jade can be a real bitch sometimes.

"I'll miss you to the moon and back," Ty says with a wink. I give both the McCabe boys a kiss on the cheek and head up the stairs to find my little sister. Not surprisingly, her door is locked, but I knock anyway and lean my forehead against the wood.

"Go away." I can barely hear her over the music blasting in the background. I have no idea what she's listening to, but it's God awful, some kind of dubstep-techno bullshit.

"It's me," I say and then pause, trying to come up with some valid reason for her to let me in. A heart-to-heart isn't exactly high on Jade's list of things to do. I consider asking for a tampon before I remember that I'm still pregnant. My stomach roils and I rest my fingers gently against the tender skin beneath my shirt. "I found some butterfly earrings on the mantle, and I thought they might be yours."

I know that Jade knows Mom was wearing butterfly earrings, that she'll do anything to get her hands on them. I hate that I'm manipulating her, but I chalk it up to tough love and let it go.

The handle twists and I step back to wait, watching as Jade sticks out a single hand, palm up.

"Give them to me," she says a split second before I shove my elbow against the door and force my way in. "What the fuck, Never?" Jade spits, shaking her head in disgust, but she doesn't try to stop me. One good thing about being a prego bitch is that everyone acts like I'm made of glass. I can pretty much get away with anything right now.

I slam the door closed behind me and flick the lock.

"There are no earrings. Sorry. Mom must've taken those along with Darla."

"Darla's missing?" Jade asks, and from the sound of her voice I can tell so many things. First, she had no idea what our mother was planning. Second, she wishes my mom had taken her instead. I glance over my shoulder and find Jade's face in a rarely seen light – a soft, aching hurt spreading there like cancer. As soon as she realizes I'm looking, it's gone, replaced with a false hardness, like an eggshell. Sure, it keeps the yolk inside, but a small tumble will send it all to shit.

"Mom took Darla," I repeat, watching as my sister turns and leans into the mirror, rubbing a bright red lipstick across her mouth. She's only twenty-one, but she looks much older right now, dressed in an old leather jacket that I'm almost positive used to belong to our mother. Jade's makeup is thick and harsh, hiding her natural beauty behind a splattered mask of cosmetics. *Fuck.* She reminds me so much of myself that it's scary. I *have* to stop this, to help her, before it's too late. I was lucky; Ty was lucky. Some people don't get so lucky. Some people don't get to live. "You didn't know anything about that, did you?"

I can see from her face that she doesn't, but she just shrugs and acts like she doesn't give a shit.

"No, I didn't, so why don't you get the hell out? Why lie to me just to come in here and bitch like Beth? I'll tell you what I told her: I already have a mom, so I don't need another one." Jade pauses and her expression shifts like a kaleidoscope. "Especially not one that disappeared without a word for five freaking years."

I close my eyes tight to gather myself. Jade is used to lashing out with hatred and anger, just so she can get some sort of reaction back. I won't give it to her; I can't.

"I hate you, Never," Jade hisses at me. "From the bottom of my heart, I hate every last inch of you."

If I let old memories take hold of me and dig their fingers in, I might as well go back to California and start sleeping around again. Things are different; *I* am different.

"Why did you tell Angelica all of the things Ty told you? I thought we were better, Jade. I thought we were doing okay. You said you were sorry, I said I was sorry, we were making progress."

Silence.

My sister says nothing, smearing ever more liner across her already glimmering lids.

I lean against her door and cringe when something sharp pokes me in the spine. It's a reindeer antler, part of some elaborately decorated wreath that would be more at home on an episode of *Hoarders* than in Noah's beautiful cabin. I wrinkle my nose at it and yank it off the nail, tossing it onto the dresser to my left. If I move away from this door, Jade will bail.

"Jade, talk to me. I know you're upset about what happened with Angelica in the living room. I saw your face."

"You don't know fucking everything, Never. You're not like a sage or something."

I sigh but force myself to take a deep breath. Jade and I have done this dance before, more times than I can even count. Our problems started before I left and they're not going to disappear just because I came back. *Sometimes, the only way to go forward, is to take a few, careful steps back.*

"What happened with Mom?" I repeat, determined to get down to the bottom of this. My sister might be stubborn, but I know I can beat her out any day. The one nice thing about taking a class at the school of hard knocks is that the tough as nails shit, that crap sticks. Even in the best of times, you get to keep it. "Did it have something to do with the photo album?"

Jade goes stone still, the hand holding her eyeliner dropping to the vanity top with a thump. She turns around to look at me in her tattered skinny jeans and her red midriff top, like she knows what she's doing, like she's totally comfortable with everything that's happening around her. Only I can see that it's all a lie.

"I see through you," I tell her. "And I love you anyway. No, actually, I love you *because* of what I see."

"Nobody loves me," Jade says, and then tears start to fall, big black streaks that cut across her rouged cheeks like swords. "Not Angelica, not Luis ... " She reaches up to brush her fingertips across the wetness on her face, like she's surprised to find it there. See what I mean? Jade's shell has just cracked, and it was that simple. See, Jade Regali wants to be loved. It really is that simple, but it's not that easy.

At least, she doesn't think it is.

For me, it's easy to love her.

"I love you, Jade," I tell her, watching as her defenses crumble and she slumps to the bed, makeup falling from her fingers like it doesn't matter anymore. I make my way over and sit down, drawing her head to my shoulder. "And whatever happened, whatever you're upset about, that's okay, too."

"I took the album, Never," she whispers. "I'm sorry. I took it because I wanted to see him again. I ... I wanted to see Dad."

When she starts to sob, I reach up and press my palm against her cheek, holding her head to me as tears tickle my own eyes. Despite the cloud of mystery surrounding my father, I think Jade is right about that one thing. He did love us. I know that now. I *remember* that now.

"Mom came in and caught me looking at it, and then she just flipped out. She said he wasn't my dad, but Never, Luis isn't my dad either." Her voice hitches on that creature's name, hinting at yet another untold story. Instead of asking about it, I hold her tighter and close my eyes, trying to get a hold of my emotions. "I hope Darla's okay," she whispers.

"I hope Darla's okay, too," I whisper back.

Knowing Angelica though, that might just be wishful thinking.

14

We welcome the New Year in with a phone call.

It's the kind everyone always dreads getting, but somehow always expects.

Lacey, Trini, Jade, and I are sitting on the couch in the living room with glasses of champagne (or in my case, sparkling apple cider) watching Ty McCabe take turns dancing with each of my little sisters. Pretty sure India, Lettie, and Lorri are all in love with him. But that's okay. In fact, I'm glad. Ty's a positive male role model and us Regalis, we could really use some more of that.

Beth answers the call when it comes in, red face stained and puffy, hand resting on her cell for a confirmation call from Zella and Noah, something that says they made it home okay, even if Angelica isn't there.

I rest my feet on bitch-Never's back, burying my toes in her fur and smile when she stretches and yawns instead of biting me. *That's a fucking first.* I take this as a good sign, of great things to come. After all, Jade and I just took another step on our journey to recovery. That, and Ty McCabe is a beautiful whirlwind of a man, my other half, my soul mate. Plus, life is made up of hills and valleys. I just plunged deep into one, said goodbye to a baby I didn't really want but that I think I kind of needed.

I turn the page of the album and brush a thumb over some singe marks.

"Hello?" Beth asks, voice wary and unfocused, like she's in another world. I'm worried about Darla, yes, but Mom managed to keep us alive all those years and we turned out okay. I think my mother's laziness will win out and we'll end up back with Darla in a very short period of time. I really don't think anything bad is going to happen. Until it does, that is. Guess I'm still in one of those valleys, and the climb up the opposite side seems like a far flung dream. "Yes, Angelica Regali is my mother."

I pause in my page turning to glance over at my sister.
Pause. Pause. Pause.
Pain.

It crashes over her in a terrible wave that chills me straight to my toes.

"Oh my God, no," she says and the wavering in her voice sends me straight to my feet. I manage to make it over to her and take the phone before it falls from her fingers.

"Hello? Miss Regali?" The voice on the other end of the line is male, unfamiliar, distant. "Hello?"

"This is Never Regali," I say, taking my old name for the sake of convenience. "Beth's sister. May I ask who this is?"

"This is Bruce Goodkind with the Mississippi State Troopers."

Fuck.

I feel the blood drain from my face.

Ty is looking right at me now, holding Lorri's hands in his, pausing right in the middle of his silly little slow dance. Our eyes meet and I start to shake.

"I'm sorry to have to give this kind of news over the phone, but there was nobody at the residence."

"We're at my friend's cabin. For Christmas," I add unnecessarily. Bruce pauses for a moment and continues on, obviously sympathetic but still very professional.

"Miss Regali, I'm sorry to have to be the one to tell you this, but we've just recovered your mother's body from the scene of an accident on I-55." I stand still and silent because I can't think of anything to say, not a single fucking thing.

My mother is dead?

"What about Darla?" I whisper, the intangible whisper of my fear nipping at the backs of my knees and forcing me to the ground. Ty's there to catch me before I hit the floor, pulling me up and hugging me to his chest. "My little sister. There should've been a little girl in the car with her."

Beside me, Beth bites back a wail and clamps her hands over her mouth. Tears stream from her too wide eyes like waterfalls, crashing against her shaking fingers and pooling on her cheeks. Somehow it feels like an eternity before the officer answers me.

I'm already too aware of all the expectant eyes facing my way, eyes who will fill with tears and drip heavy melancholy down a host of faces too young to understand that our mother wasn't worth crying over. I can't tell them their little sister is dead, too. *No, please.* Fate can't possibly be so cruel. Haven't I been dealt enough bad hands? Haven't I already paid my debts? I gave up my dignity to the cruelty of the world, gave up my father, gave up my baby.

My head spins and I have to lean even harder against Ty to stay upright.

"I apologize, ma'am," he begins and my heart explodes into a million pieces. "But we didn't find anyone else in the car."

15

I hang up the phone and turn to Beth, Ty's hands sliding off my shoulders as he waits for me to explain what's going on. I glance back at him briefly and see it in his face: he already knows. Or maybe, because we're connected by a tangled web of black decorated with stars, he can just can feel it.

"Darla?" Beth asks, and I whip my head back around to look at her. Strangely, I feel a tickle on my cheeks and reach up to find tears. I tell myself I'm only crying because I'm scared for Darla, that I don't give a crap about Angelica Regali, but I'm also nearly certain that isn't true.

"She wasn't with her," I say and Beth's face goes through a series of emotions, each one a fractured sister to the last, all of them pain and heartache and fear. "She wasn't in the car, but they're going to look for her. They want us to send some pictures in."

"What's going on?" India asks, voice wavering. I want to turn around and tell her, let the words spill from my lips, but I can't seem to move. Beth and I are just sitting there staring at one another, too shocked to move.

"Okay kiddos," Ty says, clapping his hands together in a jingle of bracelets. "Who wants to go outside and bang some pots and pans to welcome in the New Year?"

"Me, me!" Lorri shouts from behind me. Her voice is so … innocent, like bells or something. When she finds out, will that sound die away like it was never there, snatched away by the wind of fate?

"I guess," Lettie concedes as I force myself to turn and look at India and Jade, both waiting with white faces, trembling lips, tightly clenched fingers. I glance at Ty again for strength.

"We'll help, won't we, Trini?" Lacey says, standing up and dragging her girlfriend into the kitchen by the hand. Ty takes this opportunity to come over to me, bracketing my face between his hands. The bandage scrapes my face on one side while his rings brush against the other.

"It'll be okay, baby. Really, it will."

He kisses the tears from each of my eyelids and then presses a single salty peck to my lips before moving away, leaving me alone with my sisters.

"We have to find Darla," Beth whispers, her voice a trembling garble of words, barely understandable. "She could be anywhere. She could've flown through the windshield and died." Her voice rises with each word until she's nearly hysterical.

"Darla's dead?" India screeches, shaking like she's having a seizure. "No. No. No."

"Darla isn't dead!" I snap, grabbing Beth by the shoulders and squeezing until she looks up at me. Her face is barely recognizable right now, and for once, she looks her age. This, this isn't Beth the nursemaid and the nanny, the mother and the hardworking matriarch of the Regali family. This right here is twenty-four year old and terrified, overwhelmed and overworked, underappreciated Beth Ruby Regali. "Darla isn't dead," I repeat and sit down on the couch next to her. My brain is firing on all the wrong circuits right now, and I can hardly think clearly. Only ... I have to. I have to be the strong one right now and it hurts, really, really hurts. "Darla isn't dead. We'll find her, Beth." I hug my eldest sister to me and run my fingers through her tangled copper hair.

India and Jade wait for me to say something, their faces promising that they're already halfway certain they know what I'm going to say.

"Darla's okay?" India asks, but I'm not sure how to answer that question. The word *okay* is such a relative term. Is her body in the morgue with our mother? Doubtful. My guess is that Angelica dropped her off with some 'family friend' along the highway. Wouldn't be the first time.

"Darla's missing," I say. *One, two, three.* Breath. Breath. Breath. "Mom is dead."

"Mom is … ?" India begins, wrinkling her brow like she can't comprehend what it is that I'm saying. Jade, on the other hand, oh poor Jade.

"No!" she screams, sliding onto the floor on her knees. Her hazel eyes look like they've been flecked with red, bloodshot and so frightened I can hardly comprehend the depths of her pain. "No! Not my mommy. Mommy. Mommy. MOMMY!" Jade collapses to the floor and hugs herself with her arms. India tries to go to her, but she's flailing and rolling around on her back. Her screams devolve to the point where none of us can understand her anymore. "I want my mommy!" she cries again, and then I start to cry for her, falling to the floor and crawling over to her frail, shaking form.

I drag Jade's head into my lap and try to calm her down, but it doesn't work.

"I want my momma," she whimpers, snot and tears running down her face, smearing what's left of her makeup. "Bring her back. Bring my momma back."

Momma.

I try to think of a good memory, some part of Angelica that was good.

She wanted my dad dead.

And now I'll never really know if that's true.

Angelica has taken her secrets six feet under.

I can only hope she doesn't take this family with her.

16

"I want a cigarette so bad I could kill for it," I tell Ty, clutching one of my sister's Newports in my shaking fingers. I put it between my lips, but I don't smoke it. I won't fuck my baby up the way Angelica fucked up me and my sisters. "Smoke one for me," I beg, but Ty simply steals the cig from my lips and twirls it around in his ringed fingers.

"It's okay to cry," he tells me, but we both know I

know that. "It's also okay not to."

"I don't know how to feel," I admit, thinking of Jade lying on the couch with her eyes wide and empty. I'm so scared that this event is going to be her trigger, turn her into the miserable, self-hating girl that I once was. But what can I do about it? I can't bring Angelica back, can't change years of bad memories and neglect. "It's so weird losing someone you're supposed to care about, but ... but don't."

I glance over at Ty, at the silver ring between his nostrils, the perfect curve of his lips. If anyone can understand what I'm going through right now, it's him. I watch as he stares off across the lake, into the darkness and the trees that hide the world's secrets safely away from us.

"Ghosts wield great power, even from the grave," Ty says softly, tapping the cigarette against his knee in thought. I scoot a little closer to him, realizing as I do a little something about us in the action. All of the sex we have, I thought it had something to do with our addiction, like we were each other's drug. As I lay my hand over his, I wonder if it's really about closeness, if we're just so desperate to get our bodies as close as our souls already are. "I wish I could say her death might bring you some peace, but if you had to be strong before, Never, you're going to need twice that now."

Ty turns to look at me with haunted eyes, and I realize that with everything that has been happening to me, he still has issues we need to work through. Hannah and Marin Rice, and that whole fiasco, it hasn't just disappeared into thin air. I think of our house in New York and the photographs his mother took, the terrible stories from his past, and I can't help but feel a fresh set of tears beckoning.

"We are due, Ty," I tell him, squeezing his arm a little too hard. "We're due for a happy ending."

"Ah, babe, listen to me." Ty pulls me into his lap and lets the cigarette tumble to the grass beneath us. He presses our cheeks together and sighs. "You *are* my happy ending. Everything else happening around us? It doesn't mean shit."

"But I feel so … so helpless, like I can't do anything to steer my own fate."

Ty chuckles, but the sound is tinged with that old bitterness of a past life sorely lived.

"That, at least, I can help you with. See, you're thinking about things the wrong way. We're worth more than just ourselves alone, Never; we're the sum of each other. It's not you trying to steer your fate, but *us*. Let me hold half the wheel, okay?"

"I'm afraid," I whisper, putting my hands over my belly. I'm still recovering from my surgery, still suffering from the loss of my baby, and now I have to grieve the mother I never really had, too. It isn't fair.

"And that's okay, too, because, see, I love you to the moon and back. I love you farther than the stars can shine and brighter than the sun can burn. So be afraid, Never, and let me see your fears. I'll wipe them all away along with your tears."

"There is no way in fuck that you are real," I say, half-laughing and half-crying. "No fucking way. You're supposed to be a shallow bad boy with a wicked past and a good body."

"Then I have at least two of the three covered, don't

I?"

"Go to hell," I whisper, but what I really mean is *I love you.*

17

I move back inside to the sound of silence, Ty's boots and bracelets filling the empty living room like nothing else ever could. We're both tired from the frantic search for Darla that Beth put together after the phone call. It took a lot of strength to pull herself from her grief, to spread the capable and still functioning adults across the house, around the pond, in the forest, for our second search of the day – just in case Mom had turned around and dumped Darla back off without us knowing.

But we found nothing. The police even stopped in and found nothing. They took pictures and descriptions and statements, and then they left, leaving our family to survive the night alone.

Ty and I took on the burden of putting all the little ones to bed then retreated outside for a moment to pull our shit together. We're the only ones who are going to be able to do it – that much I'm sure of.

Jade has gone into shock, and both India and Beth have disappeared into their rooms, locking the doors behind them. I can hear the wails and sobs from here, but there's nothing I can do to help. I can't bring our mother back, can't make her death any less tragic for them. At this point, all I can do is keep life running smoothly – feed everyone, change diapers, prepare myself for the morning, when I'll have to tell Lettie and Lorri about Angelica. We decided that tonight, with emotions running so hot and wild, that it was best not to say anything. Ty explained away our feelings by telling them we were just worried about Darla. It was a white lie, meant to give them rest, meant to give us time, before we have to break the news. I hate to say it, but honestly, if we just never mentioned my mother again, she'd probably fade away into a distant memory in their minds. She was around so little, it probably won't make much of a difference in their lives.

Ty rests his chin on the top of my head and holds me from behind, breathing in my scent. He knows even before I do that I'm still upset, just barely holding together. Tears squeeze out and patter on the wood floor in front of me as I lift my face and turn in Ty's arms.

"I think she wanted my father dead, Ty. I think my mother ... I don't know, ordered Luis to do it or something. Paid him, bribed him, fucked him for it. Now I'll never know."

"Ignorance really can be bliss," he murmurs, holding me tight. I'm content to stay there forever when I hear a sniffle and a choke from the direction of the couch. Ty releases me, so I can go to my sister. "I'm going to go check on Noah, Autumn, and Maple," he tells me, sliding his fingers across my arm as he passes. We exchange one more look before he heads up the stairs, and I sit down beside Jade.

"Are you awake?" I ask, brushing her hair back from her face. It's a red tangle right now, like a twisted mass of copper wire.

"Leave me alone," Jade chokes as I continue to stroke her hair. I hear her words, but I also hear the meaning deep down beneath them. *Please don't go. Make things right. I'm so scared.* "I don't want another mother. I want my real mother. I want her back." Jade slaps at my hand, but that's okay. It's really okay.

She starts to break down again, choked sobs becoming violent wails, until she's struggling to breathe through the snot and the fear and the heavy, palpable weight of loss.

I sit with her until she calms down enough that I can get up, grab the phone, and take care of one last thing before bed.

Fuck.

I close my eyes and squeeze my cell in my fingers. Zella didn't *call* to say she was home safe with Noah, only texted. And so nobody here bothered to answer her. There was just too much going on.

"I don't want to do this," I whisper, but I already know that Jade is asleep, that there's nobody left to help me with this. I think maybe I should let Zella sleep, tell her tomorrow, but I'm afraid somebody else will text or call her, that she'll see it on the news first. I don't want her to find out like that.

I bite my lip and close my eyes before dialing. *Please answer. Please. Please. Please.*

"Never?" Zella sounds groggy, like she's been sleeping. It's nearly sunrise anyway, so that doesn't surprise me at all. "Are you okay?"

I have to open my eyes and stare into the dying embers of the fire before I can find my voice.

"Zella," I begin and then swallow hard. I've made a lot of difficult phone calls in my life, like the one I made to Beth that day at the clinic. This is worse. This isn't the scary beginning of something new, this is the terrible end of something horrific. "Zella, Mom got into a car accident tonight."

Silence on her end of the line.

"She ... Zella, Darla is okay. I mean, she wasn't with Angelica at the time of the accident. We don't know where she is, but she's okay." Shit. I'm stalling. I so don't want to say this, to be the one to break her heart like I did Jade's. "Mom though ... "

"She's dead," Zella says, her voice completely monotone. "Mom's dead."

I nod, even though I know Zella can't hear me.

"I have to go," she says and hangs up before I can say anything else.

I bend down low, even though it hurts my belly, and the phone falls to the floor with a clatter.

Damn you, Angelica. Just when things were looking up, when life was starting to be okay again, you had to go and do what you do best and ruin it all.

When I find myself crying again, I'm glad nobody else is around to see it.

18

Two days later and we still haven't found Darla.

A pall hangs over the Regali household, a dark shroud of a specter that taunts and whispers, showing us our worst fears and offering no relief from the pain that plagues our hearts. I've got Ty, but my sisters, they have nobody. They're all hurting too much to comfort each other and so all I see is an ocean of pain and isolated longing for a future that will never be. Now there's no more pretending that Angelica will snap to and become the mom they've always wanted. It's over. It's all really over.

"I'm so sorry about your Mom," Lacey says as we sit in the hot tub and watch the snow drift lazily from the sky, each flake like a dancer in its own right. Well, Trini, Lacey, and Ty sit in the hot tub; I sit on the edge with one foot just barely dangling in. According to Google, prego bitches shouldn't be anywhere near hot tubs or saunas. Apparently, the cells of a developing fetus get all screwy after a hundred and five degrees or so. Don't know if that's true or not, but I already lost one of my little Mini McCabes, so I'm not taking chances.

I didn't want to come out here at all at first, but when Ty and Lacey get something in their head, it's impossible to fight them both. Now I realize what a good idea this was. I'm not relaxing or hanging out, I'm rejuvenating. It felt irresponsible to sit and chat while Darla was missing and everything was falling apart, but I need this. Besides, it wasn't doing me any good to sit on the couch and stare at the phone all day. When the police call, I'll know. Anyway, Beth can barely stand, so someone has to take over her role; I could use a moment to recuperate some of my strength for that reason alone. Of course, Ty is taking care of the babies and the kids like only a true prince could ever do. Yes, his crown might be made of thorns, but his heart is purer than pure, broken and bent into a shape that's so much better than what we all start out with.

"Thank you, Lacey," I say, staring back at her blonde hair and blue eyes, her perfect Barbie face. Trini sits beside her while Ty sits beside me, the four of us lapsing into contemplative silence for a while. I feel bad for them, coming all the way out here for a Christmas that sucked worse than my first blow job. I tell Lacey this and she gives me a raised brow.

"Sorry? Don't be sorry, Never. None of this is your fault."

"Yeah, but, what a way to spend a holiday, huh?" I say, and Ty reaches out of the water to squeeze my hand.

"Holidays are about family, and I think I've learned more about that in the time I've been here than I have the rest of my life combined. I mean, I'm not saying my family doesn't love each other or anything, but you and your sisters ... you and *Ty*," Lacey makes an inappropriately lascivious face that makes me smile, just a little, "you're so real. You feel so much. I feel like it's hard to say how strong a family's bonds are until they're tested. Well, yours have been and still are. That's the mark of true strength, Never."

I look away because I'm not used to compliments like that. My family. We're really like that? I find it hard to believe. We're so broken and fractured and now, who knows what will happen to us?

"Did you read that in a Hallmark card?" I ask and Ty chuckles softly.

"Nope. It's just the truth, plain and simple. You'll have to deal." Lacey pauses and she and Trini exchange a long look. I remember the night they first met, how I crawled into Lacey's car and cried myself to sleep. I really have come a long way. "We, uh, have something to tell you, but it didn't seem appropriate considering everything. I mean, I know Darla's still missing and all, but since we're leaving tomorrow ... " Lacey trails off and takes a deep breath. "Trini and I are getting married, and we wanted you to be the first ones to know."

"Congrats, doll," Ty says, moving across the hot tub to give Lacey a totally inappropriate hug. At least I know she's gay and getting absolutely nothing from his bare chest brushing up against her. "That's fucking sweet. When and where are you doing the deed?"

"We're not sure," Trini says, brushing some dark hair behind her ear. I don't know her as well as I do Lacey, but I've always liked her and I've always appreciated how good she's been to my friend – my *only* female friend if you don't count my sisters. "But we were hoping you guys could come. Maybe even be a part of it?"

"I'd love to," I say, remembering that white dress with the red ties that Ty bought me. That we fucked in. An idea of a real wedding seems so far away right now, but I grab onto it and cling because weddings, as silly as I think they are, are a sign of hope, a sign that the future isn't bleak and empty. I think Lacey and Trini know that, that they're telling me this now, here, on purpose. Not to be callous about Darla's plight or to gloat about their relationship or anything like that, just to keep me hopeful.

It doesn't last long.

My mother is dead.

I force that thought back again, fully aware that it'll resurface in a matter of minutes. Welcome to my life for the past few days. What with the funeral and will and custody crap, what with fucking Darla missing, I *need* this. And anyway, we'll find Darla soon, I'm sure of it. We *have* to find her or my family won't survive. I choke back the emotions and blink away the tears, forcing myself to stay positive, keep my voice lighthearted.

"But I won't wear an ugly bridesmaid dress." Lacey giggles, but I don't give in. "Seriously. Don't forget we used to be roommates. I can't banish some of the atrocities you wore from my mind."

"Pink cashmere is not an atrocity," Lacey says, but even Ty has to smile at that one. "Okay, fine, think what you want, but I promise, no pink cashmere at my wedding. Deal?"

I smile back.

"Deal."

19

Where the fuck is Darla?

That's the million dollar question right now, one that's eating away at my sisters' already fragile souls. India, Jade, and Beth, I don't think a single one of them has eaten in days. And Zella? After my initial phone call to tell her the news, we haven't heard from her. I can only hope Noah Scott is taking good care of her. Even if she's stubborn about it, I know he will.

He'll find a way. Love always does.

"I've tried everyone in her contacts list," Beth says, setting aside my mother's phone like it's a precious heirloom and not a scratched up hunk of junk. "All of the friends and boyfriends and pot dealers that I could possibly remember from a fucking lifetime of shit." Beth drops her head into her hands, copper hair tangled and ratted. She won't brush it and she won't let anyone else touch it either. When she starts to cry again, I pull my knees up to my chest and close my eyes.

Seven days.

That's a long time to lose track of someone, especially someone who's four years old and precocious as hell.

I open my eyes again and look at India, head down, tears streaming over her cheeks. It's hard to decide what each emotion means, how my sisters are really feeling. If Darla were here, would they still be this upset? I know Jade would, but India and Beth? I don't know. I can't talk about our mother with them, can't process what's happened, because the only thing that matters right now is finding our sister. It's like we're stuck in this terrible limbo, this purgatory of what-ifs and who-knows. Darla could be dead – worse. I try really, really hard not to think of Marin Rice in that moment.

"Pancakes, anyone?" Ty asks, mostly looking at me. I haven't been eating as much as I should, I know that. I nod, even though I'm not hungry. I'll eat, but only for my baby and not for myself. "I can even make 'em in the shape of Mickey Mouse or some shit. Ooh, that sounds good, doesn't it?"

Beth sniffles, but at least she actually looks up at him with a loose smile on her pretty mouth.

"Mickey Mouse pancakes are Darla's favorite," she says, and then she breaks down in sobs again. Ty cringes and sets his spatula down, moving over to pull my big sister against his belly. I watch as he strokes her hair with ringed fingers. Only ... he's looking right at me. I look right back and something passes between us. I remember his words from a few weeks back. *Love is glue, baby. Without it, sometimes the cracks begin to show.*

"Don't cry, Mother Dearest," he says and I smile at the affectionate lilt to his voice. Despite the fact that they're only a year apart in age, Ty really does see Beth as a mother figure. "I can make pancakes in the shape of penises, too, if that's what you'd prefer."

"God no," Beth chokes out, pulling away and smoothing some hair behind her ears with her fingers. "That's the absolute last thing I could ever want or need. Make Mickey Mouse pancakes. Maybe they'll bring us some luck? Besides, Never is way too skinny."

I roll my eyes, but only for normalcy's sake.

"I'm, like, ten weeks along or something," I say, but Beth isn't listening. Over the baby monitor, somebody cries. Honestly, I can't tell if it's Autumn or Mini McCabe.

"I'll get 'em," India says suddenly, shoving her chair out from the table and disappearing through the entrance to the living room. She barely makes it out before fresh tears start falling. Fuck. I wish there was something more I could do, something better. Instead, all I've been able to do is sit here and wish and hope and pray like everyone else.

"How are you feeling, honey?" Beth asks, sniffling

again and shifting things around on the table. She organizes the place settings, moving forks and knives and spoons by mere fractions of an inch. If her OCD tendencies will help her feel better, I'm not going to say anything. "I mean, are your incisions healing alright?"

"I think so," I say and she snaps her gaze up to mine. "Yes. Sorry. Yes, they look fine. And I have a checkup on Monday, so don't look at me like that." Beth nods and then goes quiet, like that was all the mothering and nagging she had left in her. I wet my lips for a moment and then decide to bring up things I'm sure she'd rather leave buried. "Beth." Something about the way I say her name draws her attention to me. Tears are flowing again, but somebody has to bring this stuff up. "What are we going to do with Mom's body?"

"Do?" Beth asks, sounding strangled. "I'll tell you what I *did*. I told the fucking hospital to cremate her and throw the ashes in the trash!" She stands up suddenly and shoves her chair so hard it topples and smashes into the wall. "I told them to make sure she went straight to fucking hell where she belongs!" My sister's screams turn into sobs, but when I stand up and try to go to her, she pulls away. "Don't touch me!" she wails, stumbling away and leaning into the wall like the world is so heavy on her shoulders she couldn't possibly stand. "Do you understand how bad this is? I'm twenty-four, Never. Twenty-fucking-four. I have two babies and no husband, no father, no mother. I have fucking *nothing*."

I reach out a hand but Beth slaps it away. She's on a rant now and there's nothing I can do to stop her.

"We are orphans, Never. Orphans. My sister, basically my daughter, is missing, and I can't do shit about it. I have no money, can only pray that I get custody of the girls, can only fucking hope that I get the house."

Beth sits down heavy on the floor and stops only when Ty presents a plate to her, Mickey Mouse pancake smiling up from a sea of butter and maple syrup. She stares at it for a long moment before finally reaching out and taking it.

"Thanks."

I look over at my husband. He winks and salutes me before going back to his cooking. This guy, this damaged little bad boy of mine, apparently he's just this good at taking care of broken girls. Or maybe broken people in general? Ty really should become a therapist or a psychologist or a social worker or what-the-fuck-ever because I think he could heal a little piece of the world, one butterfly armed hug at a time, one well-placed bit of advice smattered with the F-bomb. Ah, Ty.

"I think we should have a funeral," I say, even though I can't believe the words are slipping past my suddenly dry lips. Then again, funerals aren't for the dead but for the living. My sisters, especially my little sisters, I think they need this. Beth, whether she wants to admit it or not, needs this.

"We can't afford a funeral, Never," Beth mutters, but at least she's eating her pancake. That's something, isn't it?

"We can't afford to dress in black, dig a hole out back and put Angelica's ashes to rest?"

Beth says nothing, but that's okay. I can take care of this for her because I'm the strong one now. Not sure when that happened, but I can see that it's true. Beth needs me, needs Ty; she needs *us*.

20

Listening to the gravel ping against the windows of Beth's minivan is hard for me, almost too hard. Old memories reach up like a sea of undead hands from the grave, grabbing at the loose layers of black that flow around my ankles. I'm wearing one of India's dresses because I haven't got any of my own, not any that would be appropriate or that wouldn't hurt. Waistbands and tight fitting shirts are still agony for me, rubbing against my belly and reminding me at every possible moment that life isn't easy, nor is it black and white. Life is a million shades – but not of gray. No, I've learned that whole *shades of gray* crap is bullshit. Life is all color, whether it's good or bad. It's a fucking rainbow that shoots across the sky and bathes everything in light. Yes, I lost one baby, but I discovered another.

Zella is waiting in front of the house, a nippy midwest wind tugging at her hair and whipping it around her face. It's blonde now, much like that of the boy that stands beside her, close but not too close.

As soon as Ty stops the car, I'm out the door and closing my eyes against the sight of the old farmhouse, against the memories. The gravel hurts my bare feet, but in a way, it also feels good, like no sensation right now could be a bad sensation. It just is. *I* just am.

"I know I said I liked you barefoot and pregnant, but this is taking it a little too far, don't ya think?" Ty scoops me up in his arms like I weigh nothing, like I'm simply a swallowtail alighting on his muscular arm. "The ground is frozen as fuck, babe. And seriously, I *really* like your toes. If you lost some to hypothermia, we wouldn't be able to do all those weird little foot fetish things I've never tried."

"I didn't know you had a foot fetish," I tell him, putting a hand on his chest and feeling the beat of his black, bloody heart. He raises his pierced brow at me.

"I don't, not really. I just like everything about you. You're my fetish."

I smile and lean in for a kiss, just a quick one though. It feels wrong to make out on a day like this, especially since Darla is still missing. My worry for her has twisted into a thin snake of ice in my gut. I try to ignore it, but it refuses to be left alone. The cops have promised they're looking for her, but how, when even we don't know where to start looking? We're her family, so we should have some idea at least.

"I'm ... glad you guys are back," Zella whispers as Ty carries me over to the porch and sets me down on the bottom step. She reaches up and subconsciously fiddles with her freshly colored hair. "It was lonely here without everyone, but I thought, maybe, if I waited that Darla might show up somehow."

I nod, but there's nothing I can say to make things better, so I turn around and watch as Ty jogs back to the van to grab our son and help the rest of the kids out. Beth is barely there inside her own head, eyes distant and a scary sort of vacant. She clutches the box of our mother's ashes to her chest, but forgets to get Autumn and Maple out of their carseats. Nobody mentions the empty seat in Jade's car, the one where Darla should've been sitting.

"Let's get this fucking over with," Beth says, her voice a monotone. I exchange a look with Zella before slipping inside the house and grabbing some boots. There's a big, black pair of worn, dirty combat boots that Ty left here before we took off for the cabin. I slip my feet inside, feeling small when the shoes sag and slip around as I make my way back outside.

India has a shopping bag on her arm, filled with candles, and a bouquet of flowers in the opposite hand. It's not much, but then again, my mother doesn't really deserve anything other than a scowl and some spit. Honestly, I would hock one on her grave if I thought it would help. It won't. I know that now. *Even if she did have my father killed.* Too bad the truth will forever remain a mystery. Unless, I suppose, I ask Luis. The chances of getting anything out of that rapist/murderer though is slim to none.

Ty has Little Noah in the Sharpie bullet baby carrier, so I slip my hand through his, letting his rings kiss my skin with warm metal. We swing them between one another as we make our way between the house and the barn, past the tractor where Ty and I made love, until we stop in a bit of dead, frozen grass. The property is mostly flat with hardly any trees, so there's not really a 'good' place to bury Momma. All we can do is choose a random spot, a final resting place for a woman I should be devastated over losing, should be crushed by missing. Only I don't. All I want right now is Darla. All I want is for my family to be fucking whole.

"I dug as deep as I could," Noah says as we pause beside a fairly shallow hole. It's carved into the flat, midwestern earth like a scar, like the earth is gaping in an openmouthed frown. "But the ground is frozen, solid as a rock." He pauses next to the pile of dirt and runs his tongue across his lower lip. Zella watches him for a moment and then looks away. Christ, if all of this shit going down can't spur these two idiots to deal with their differences, I don't know what will. Life is too damn short. Look at our bitch mother. She screwed around and lazed about like she didn't have a care in the world, shirked her love and her responsibilities, and now she's about to be buried in a foot deep whole, trapped in a cardboard box for the rest of eternity. I mean, *if* she has a soul – which is doubtful – then this can be her personal hell, to watch the family she should've loved from afar, never again to touch or hold or speak to any of us. Maybe then she can finally learn her lesson?

"You want me to dig deeper?" Ty says, and the words send a chill down my spine. Or maybe it's the icy January wind, nipping at my bare arms as I cross them over my chest.

"No," Beth says firmly, stepping forward and gripping the box with fingers so tight they look like bone. "This is good enough."

"Can I pass out the candles?" India asks, looking over at my little sisters, Lettie and Lorri. Their faces are drawn and puffy, little tear stains cutting across their cheeks. They're young enough that maybe, just maybe, they'll remember our mother in some sort of falsely brilliant light. Good. I don't ever want them to know her many faults, how she was the Evil Stepmother from all the fairytales without even being a *step* anything. I don't want them to know that sometimes, a bad guy can be a super villain without beating anyone or hurting them sexually, that the mental torture and the feeling of abandon can be just as bad.

Beth says nothing, so I take the flowers from India's hand while she passes out a few white taper candles. Jade is holding Autumn, so she doesn't take one, but I can see she desperately wants to, so I switch her out mine for my niece, bringing the baby's sweet smelling head to my lips for a kiss. Maple clings to Beth's skirt, but in some strange parody of my mother, Beth ignores her. It hurts my heart, but I know it's only temporary, born out of grief and fear.

Once the candles are lit, clutched close and protected

with open palms against the wind, Beth steps forward
and sets the box in the ground. I think I see a single tear
hit the cardboard lid before she stands up, but I can't be
sure.

"Does anyone have anything they want to say?" Beth
drawls, a slight Southern accent creeping into her words.
I hardly ever hear it, but it's there now.

"Don't you?" Jade asks, her voice high-pitched and on
the verge of hysteria. "She was our *mother.*"

"Yeah, and because of her actions, Darla is gone.
What could I possibly say right now that would be
appropriate?" Beth raises her brows at Jade and purses
her lips. "Do you want me to talk about the fact that our
mother got engaged to a murderer, that she drove her
own daughter away?" Beth points at me, and my throat
closes up. Fuck. Jade already has a target on my back,
uses me as an emotional punching bag. This? This is
only going to make that worse. "That she had *eight*
children with six different men? That she barely made
enough money to feed us, sold our food stamps for cash,
and disappeared at the worst times possible?"

Jesus.

Jade's face lights with a fury I've never seen, not even
on the night I ran away, when she told me she hated me.

"Take it back," she growls, stepping forward, right up
to the edge of the hole that is our mother's grave. "Take
it all back!"

"Why?" Beth asks, nonchalant, broken, her spirit in
tatters and hanging around her like a desecrated flag.
"It's all true."

Jade moves forward, but I stop her with a hand on her
arm.

"Angelica Regali was a master of tribal belly dance, with over twenty years of experience under her belt. She was the mother of eight gorgeous daughters, and grandmother to three and a half beautiful babies." I put my hand on my belly and take a deep breath. These are some of the most difficult words I've ever spoken, each one like a piece of glass cutting across my lips, but that's okay. To heal, sometimes you have to bleed first. "She made mistakes, but she was human, and capable of great things."

I dig as deep as I can for that elusive spirit we all have inside of us: forgiveness. Fuck, but it's hard. I push aside years of neglect and frustration and I find something, just a little something to tell. Hopefully it's enough.

"I remember how when Beth, Jade, Zella and me were little, after teaching her dance class at the community center, Mom would take us to the little diner by the railroad tracks. We'd order one mammoth sized ice cream sundae to share, and then we'd all get sick after." Jade chuckles and sniffles, so I know I'm on the right track here. "It must've been because back then, all she ever fed us were veggie burgers on toast. And sometimes, after we crawled into bed and she thought we were asleep, you could hear Mom singing *Black Velvet* in the living room."

I take a huge breath and glance over at Ty. He's looking right at me, lips curved in the most perfect smile. *I am worth it.* I look back over at the pile of dirt and move towards it slowly, Ty's boots crunching across the ground beneath my feet. Reaching down, I grab a handful of frozen rocks and soil and turn to look at my mother, one, last time.

I forgive you.

I toss my handful on the box and say my final goodbye.

"You know," Ty whispers as I rejoin him on the opposite side of the hole, leaning down to breathe hot and warm against my ear, "you have the biggest fucking heart I've ever seen, read, or dreamed about."

"Even if it's as dark as the night sky?"

"Especially because of that."

21

Ty's silly tabby cat molests him while I watch from the opposite side of the bed, glaring at the beast from hell with narrowed eyes. Chuck Norris won't stop rubbing his cheek against my husband's lip ring, and kneading the ever living crap out of his bare chest. Ty indulges the behavior and gives me a look with both brows raised.

"You look a little bit jealous," he says, wrapping

the cat in his beautiful arms, pressing a kiss to the top of its head.

"Of a cat?"

"The only pussy he can have is mine, is what you're thinking. Come on, just fess up and spill. I get it, babe."

I roll my eyes, but it feels good to be sitting here with him, cloaked in the darkness of my old bedroom with our dog sleeping by our feet and our son in his crib. If we can exchange witty banter, the world's not completely gone to shit, right?

"You okay?" he asks when I don't respond right away. I look down at my pajama pants, the red and black striped zebra ones that I've had for forever and a day. I pick at a hole with my fingernail and then glance back up. Ty's hair is mussy and disheveled, but in the most perfect way, like he styled it to look like that in the first place. And who knows with him, maybe he did? His tattoos glow in low light like this, pop off his skin until I'm halfway fucking sure they're going to take flight and flutter over to me, land on my eyelashes and press little butterfly kisses to my cheeks. In memoriam of my late mother, he's wearing all black piercings, rings, and bracelets today. I like the contrast against his skin, the clatter of glass as he reaches over with his smoky black bangles and touches the side of my face.

"I'm ... I think I would be if Darla were here, Ty. Is that wrong? Is it wrong that I don't miss my mother? I feel like I've already cried a sea of salt for that woman. I just don't feel like I have anything left in me."

"Totally normal, natural, and perfectly expected." Ty brushes my hair back and I sigh, leaning into his touch. "Blood is absolutely not fucking thicker than water.

Sure, that shit can stain like nobody's business, but that doesn't mean it has to dictate everything. Angelica was your mother, sure, but she lost her chance with you last year, Never. When you fight against everything inside of you to extend an olive branch to someone, and they snap it in half, it's hard to make things right. Angelica didn't *want* to make things right with you."

"I feel guilty is all," I say with a sigh, but Ty is having none of that. He sits up and scoots over, gently sliding his arm around my waist, so he can tug me down to the pillows before leaning over and flicking off the light. We're plunged into moonlit darkness, but I don't care. I'm at home in the dark. The little monster inside of me lived here once and even though I evicted her bitch ass, I still know my way around.

"Guilt is a disease best left cured. Don't let it eat you alive, babe. I'm a selfish asshole, me. I want all of you to myself. Each hole that fucker eats is one less piece I get to ravage at night." Ty kisses my ear and I shiver, my entire body lighting up like a firecracker on the 4th of July. *Jesus fuck.* Only, like, five freaking weeks to go. Shit. We're never going to make it. "Besides, guilt cripples people like nobody's business. Get up, give fate a rabbit punch to the throat, and move on."

I burrow into Ty's side, breathe his scent in and let it coat my lungs. This, this is how I want to die, lying next to the love of my life with the gritty perfection of bad boy and cigarettes and fucking soap filling my nostrils. I'll die happy then, truly I will.

"Will you still love me when I'm old and wrinkled?" I whisper randomly. Everybody has these thoughts at some point, don't they? I have no idea why I decide to ask this question at this exact moment, but I do. Maybe it's because I know Ty will give me the answer I want to hear. What I don't say, but that he probably already knows, is that lying next to him like this is the most soothing balm my twisted soul could ever ask for. Sleeping next to a guy, knowing him, *not* fucking him. It's the most intimate thing I've ever done. And the fact that I have Ty's baby inside of me? My stomach explodes into a swarm of butterflies, and I actually feel *nervous* being around him, excited. I hope this feeling never fades.

Ty pulls me just a little bit closer, hugs me a little tighter.

"I'll love you *because* you're old and wrinkled. Nev, some people get freaked out at the thought of being old, but you know what? If you get that far, you should just consider yourself lucky. I'd rather die old and toothless in your arms than drop dead tomorrow. Sure, I'd leave a pretty corpse, but it wouldn't be worth it. Each second with you is a fucking gift."

I laugh, lifting up his shirt with my left hand, so I can lay my fingers against bare skin.

"You're too much, you know that? Do you come up with this shit on the fly or plan your lines in advance?"

"Um, I'm a bad boy, remember? I got lines for days, baby cakes." Ty presses a kiss to my forehead and then quickly moves his lips down to mine for a deeper taste. "And tomorrow," he continues, still kissing me, punctuating his words with hot, quick bursts of his beautiful mouth. "I'm going ... " Ty's tongue slides across my bottom lip. "To find ... " Just a bit of teeth, a nip that leaves me gasping and arching my back. Have I ever been kissed quite like this? No. The answer is no fucking way. "Your ... " The little devil pushes my arms back into the bed when I try to reach for him.

"Please say clitoris," I moan, but he only kisses me harder, shushing me.

"No, your sister." I pause and so does Ty, looking down at me in the dark. I notice how the asshole has somehow draped himself just so over my upper body, just enough that he can hold my arms down, kiss me, tease me, but without hurting me.

"How?" I ask, because Darla's disappearance is a mystery that doesn't seem to want to be solved. What would my mom do with her? Where would she take her?

"I don't know yet, but I'm going to figure this shit out. I can't sit around and watch you all fall apart. Besides, I love the fuck out of that kid." Ty's voice sounds strained, worried. I know what he went through in his past, watching his cousin being abused, being abused himself, and I can see that even though he's playing calm, he's terrified for Darla. I bite my lower lip. I don't think I've quite admitted to myself how scared I am, too. "But we'll find her. I know we fucking will."

Ty drops his mouth to mine again, fierce and powerful, the other half I've always wanted, always so desperately needed. I try to pull my hands from his grip, but he won't let me, keeping me pinned with one bandaged hand and one ringed one. *He went through flames for me.* Like a sign from above, my chip earring catches beneath me, tugging on my ear and reminding me about everything we've been through together, everything we've survived together.

Ty's mouth is all pressure right now, just lips and

molten hot heat. I'm already losing my head, getting swept away in him, in my addiction. Or no. No, not necessarily that. Ty and me, we just need to be close, especially right now. I arch against him, but he stays firm, keeping me pressed into the bed with sheer force, his muscles tight, keeping him up and off of my injured belly. It's enough to drive me fucking nuts. I'm not used to being denied. My libido *really* isn't used to being denied.

I try to tell Ty that this is torture, but he won't let me speak, sliding his tongue across my lower lip again, eating my words away. He nips and bites at my swollen flesh as I moan against him, thrashing in his grip. When his tongue runs up the side of my face, over to my ear, I practically scream. He takes the chip earring in his teeth and tugs on it gently.

"You're so strong, Never. It's one of the many, many things I love about you."

"Stop it," I growl back at him, but he doesn't care. Ty never gives a shit about what other people think. And that, that is one of the many, many things I love about *him.* "You're giving me blue balls, asshole."

He snorts, but doesn't bother to pull away, bringing his mouth back to mine. This time he gives me all he's got – tongue and teeth and the hottest, hungriest wolfish lips.

"I want to fuck you so bad, baby. I want to bury myself inside of you and take away all of this pain." Ty lets go of my arms and I throw them around his neck, burying my fingers in his beautiful, black hair while he nuzzles my throat and groans low and deep. The sound travels through his chest and into me, making me shiver.

When he lifts his face back to mine, sighs against my lips, I come completely undone.

I raise up to kiss him, moaning into his mouth, drawing more sounds of desperation and desire from the man I love more than life itself. Just when I think I can't take it anymore, that I'm going to die if we don't at least *try* to fuck each other, I hear a knock at my door.

Ty and I exchange a look, but he carefully untangles himself from me and pads over to answer it.

Lorri stands in the hallway, face cloaked with tears, copper hair tangled and mussy.

"I can't sleep without Darla," she whispers through a half-sob. "I miss her."

"Aw, honey." Ty pulls my sister into the room and helps her into the bed. "We'll find her, sweetie. I can promise you that. Here, you sleep with your sister and I'll sleep in your bed."

"Don't you dare leave me," I whisper as I help Lorri climb under the covers. I point to the spot behind me. "You can sleep here."

"Oh trust me, love, if I *could,* I absolutely would. But right now, it wouldn't be appropriate for me to lay next to you and your sister thinking the things that are running through my head." He winks at me once, kisses me quick on the lips and disappears into the hallway. We keep eye contact until the door shuts fully behind him.

I sigh softly, releasing my feelings of sexual frustration and putting them aside for my sister. We curl up together then and fall asleep to the sound of the wind whistling across the icy ground outside my window.

And all I dream about is Ty.

22

Week two of no Darla, and it's starting to feel like the new year is bust, like there's no point in even trying to make resolutions or change things, no point in trying to smile or pretending to be happy. It's past the point where we're certain our late mother has just dropped her off somewhere and starting to get to the point where we all know something is wrong.

"I passed out all the flyers," Ty says as I stare down at

the silent telephone on the kitchen table and wonder if we'll ever get a call – from the police, from an old family friend, from anyone at all really. The cops have a tip line set up, but nobody's called in except once when India made the mistake of taking Maple to the grocery store with her. Somebody saw them and tore my niece from my sister's arms, convinced she was Darla.

Told you we all look alike.

"I swear, at this point, I feel like I've met everybody in this town at least once. The lady at the dry cleaner's, the one with the bright pink hair and the cowboy boots, man, she must be at least ninety years old and she won't stop pinching my ass."

"Actually," I say, smiling despite myself. "She turned a hundred last year. It was the top story on the town's website."

"This watering hole has a website?" Ty asks, looking down at me and cupping the side of my face in firm but gentle fingers. I know he knows that my smile is fake, that if I had dimples like him they wouldn't be showing right about now.

"Welcome to Podunk, USA," I say with another sigh. My smile disappears and all I can think about is Darla and the ripple effects of her missing from our lives. Beth is trashed; India is broken; Zella won't stop sleeping in her car. Every night, after she thinks we're all asleep, Jade goes downstairs and sits by our mother's makeshift grave. I can see her from my window, lips moving as she carries on a silent conversation with a ghost. It's sad, but I can't bring myself to do anything about it.

All I can do is this.

I've made a website for Darla, a Facebook page, even

a Twitter. I've spoken to every missing child advocacy agency in the state, maybe the country. I call the police station at least three times a day, even if I'm sure there's nothing to report. I've even gone through every piece of paper in the house, called every phone number I could find, tracked down every person. And last night, Ty and I stopped over at the Broken Glass, that shit hole scum dwelling bar, and waited outside for Luis. We even followed him back to his place and watched him go inside from the street. When the lights went dark, Ty slipped out and broke in – a trick he says he learned back in the day, when it was survival of the fittest – and looked around.

No Darla.

"You feelin' okay?" Ty asks, making pouty lips at me because he knows I'm going to get defensive. I shouldn't, but I do anyway. I can't help it. I've been taking care of myself for so long that sometimes it just feels wrong to let someone else do it for me.

I splay my fingers out across midsection. With Darla's very real and very obvious absence, I haven't had a chance to think much about the missing twin in my belly. I wonder if Ty and I will tell our new child that they had another half? Not anytime soon, of course, but later.

"The doctor said I was," I mumble as he leans down and grabs the seat of my chair, pulling it out from under the table and turning it, so he can look me right in the face. Ty leans in close, the bracelets on his arms ringing like bells, and breathes against my ear.

"No bullshit, Nev. I almost lost you." Ty's trying to keep his voice light, but he chokes a little when he says this. I can't even imagine what he must've gone through while I was in surgery. I've tried asking him about it, but the pale color of his skin and the sweat that beads on his forehead usually deters me from delving very deep into it. "I want to know everything. I want to know how many times you took a piss today, if you threw up, what you ate. Everything."

"Are you trying to get all alpha male on my ass?" I joke, leaning back and giving him a *look*. "Because you know I don't respond well to that shit. When I said I liked bad boys, I meant rock stars and erotic dancers, not CEOs and motorcycle club presidents."

Ty laughs, but the sound is restrained, like we're in a padded room and the walls are absorbing all the noise. That's how the whole house feels actually. Stuffy. Desperate. Afraid.

"If that's a hint, then I totally didn't need it. Check this out."

Ty stands up and moves over to the window seat. He'd dropped a cloth shopping bag there on his way in, the one he'd used to hold all the flyers, but I didn't think much of it. Now, when he returns to me, I see there's something inside.

"Open it," he says, eyes sparkling. He's too cute with his brown eyes and crooked smile, so I do what he asks and find an eReader, a brand spanking new one.

"Ty, this is too much," I say, but he's already shaking his head.

"Nothing is too much except maybe my love for you. There's so much of it that I'm literally exploding." He pats his chest and tosses me a wink right about the same moment that India walks in.

"Please don't talk about exploding on my sister in front of me."

Ty just laughs and moves away like the gift means nothing, but me? I have to blink rapidly to clear away tears. I won't cry over something as silly as this, not when Darla's out there alone. But Ty must've used the very, very last of his fuck money to buy me this because he knew I needed a distraction.

I feel my heart start to pound and my mouth go dry.

I love him.

Oh God, I love him.

More than I can even define by the laws of nature. After all, infinite is an impossible concept, isn't it?

"Any news?" India asks, tucking her long copper hair behind one ear. Her hazel eyes are sparkling, and her voice hitches with so much hope that I almost wish I could lie to her, tell her we've had a promising lead come through.

Instead I shake my head no.

The kitchen goes silent for a while as I run my fingers over the eReader's box, wishing all I had to care about right now was being pregnant and diving into a good book. Honestly, all I really want to do is dive into one anyway, let myself get lost in another world so I can forget how harsh around the edges this one can be sometimes.

At least I have Ty. He's my blur tool, the button I can click to smooth out all the sharp lines and breaks in life, make everything look soft and fuzzy even if it's not.

I check out his ass while he digs around in the cabinets looking for something to eat. Considering he's the only person 'round here that's done any shopping, I feel like I should be making something for him. Bastard that he is, he won't let me. I keep telling him his 'white knight' is starting to show.

"Mac 'n' cheese, mac 'n' cheese, or mac 'n' cheese?" Ty asks, glancing over his shoulder. "That's pretty much all we have left. I didn't have time to stop at the store today." I shake my head because I hate how much responsibility has been heaped on him lately, afraid that he's going to stumble or trip or fall. It's not that I think he's weak or anything. No, not at all. Ty and me, we were never weak. It's just … this is a lot for anyone to have to deal with, let alone someone who's just starting to learn to be a real person again.

"Mac 'n' cheese is perfect," I tell him, and I mean it, too.

India slumps into a chair beside me.

"We have to go back to school tomorrow," she says, sweeping her hair back and grabbing the sides of her face. "I don't know how I'm going to sit there all day and not think about Darla."

"Leave the worrying to me," I tell her, reaching out and peeling her fingers away from her cheek. "Concentrate on school, and I'll find our sister."

"What about you?" she asks suddenly, making my stomach queasy. "Aren't you supposed to be going back to school, too?"

I pause for a moment and think about the U, about living with Lacey and going to class and meeting Ty for the first time. I get all twisted and tongue-tied until I can't even think up a single decent thing to say.

I met you in a bar. We stopped a robbery together. We got tested. We went to SOG.

We fell in love.

"We're enrolled for Spring term. Doesn't start until the end of March," Ty says, reaching into his back pocket like he's going for a cigarette. Thing is, he doesn't have any. As far as I know, Ty has gone completely cold turkey with me.

"What are you talking about?" I ask, because the closest university is almost two hours away. Locally, there's nothing but the community college. And besides, getting in as a new student during spring term is almost impossibly difficult.

"I wrote a letter to the dean of admissions explaining your situation."

I blink several times and curl my fingers up inside the sleeve of my black hoodie. I have to, to hide the shaking.

"What? When the hell would you have time to do all that?"

"While you were sleeping," Ty says, turning around with a piece of red licorice between his lips, like it's the cigarette I'm sure he's dreaming about. "Remember when I was ordering your transcripts? Well, I sent the email off right before that. So, guess what, baby? You're in." Ty snaps his ringed fingers. "Oh, and they've got a very impressive online class catalogue." He eyes my still flat belly. "You know, in case you're not able to make it to campus."

I'm just sitting there staring, openmouthed and in complete shock.

"What about you?" India asks, glancing over at him. Ty shrugs like it doesn't matter, but I see a spark of determination in his eyes, and it is beyond brilliant.

"I'm actually going to go to the community college

first, get my general ed shit out of the way. I already filled out my *FAFSA*," Ty says, giving me a wink. If he's like me – which I know he is – then he's remembering the first time I ever mentioned that to him. *Free Application for Federal Student Aid.*

I feel like we're coming full circle and it's breathtaking. If only Darla were here to share it with us. Darla, Darla, Darla.

Fuck.

"I've got some good grants and whatnot, work study and all that. They even have a daycare there that I can use for free if I put in some hours."

"You've really got your shit together, huh?" India asks at the same moment Ty's cell buzzes. He fishes it out of his pocket with a perplexed expression on his face. Understandable since the only people that call him are Beth and Lacey. The former is curled upstairs in bed, processing the news that both the sweep of the pond at Noah's cabin, and the massive community walkthrough of the forest uncovered nothing. I took it as a good sign, elated to hear that my sister's body wasn't sitting in the bottom of a lake or lying in the woods somewhere, but Beth was still upset.

And Lacey, I know she and Ty talked just a few hours ago. So who is it?

I watch Ty's face shift from confused to enraged within a matter of seconds.

"Who is it?" I ask him, desperate to know, terrified to find out.

He looks up at me, butterfly fingers clutching the phone, brown eyes flashing.

"It's Hannah."

23

Ty holds a cigarette in bejeweled fingers, bracelets clinking as he brings it to his lips for a drag. His left hand holds his cell and his booted foot taps out a rhythm of discontent on the porch. I stand to his left, just in front of the screen door, keeping an eye out for eavesdroppers.

"Sorry about the smoke," he says, gazing down at the burning cherry with a frown plastered across his perfect lips. I shake my head and pull Ty's coat closer around me. It smells like him, like bad boys and hearts that were once broken but are now healed. Ty's scent. It comforts me now just as it did at the clinic all those many months ago.

"With all of this stress, I'm surprised you even lasted this long." He looks over at me with a ghostly smile hovering above his mouth, like he wishes he could be happy but can't. It makes me sad. And frustrated. And so mad that I feel like I could march upstairs to my mom's old bedroom, take the shotgun that's in her closet, and go take care of Hannah forever.

Hannah.

My mouth twists down in a scowl. That fucking pedophile. Here. In my town. It makes me sick to my stomach to even think about it. As far as I'm concerned, she raped Ty. It's at least partially her fault that he had to go through all of that shit. *She* is at fault for the whole Marin Rice thing. Her. I fucking hate her so much I can barely breathe.

"Only one, I swear," Ty says lifting up both palms in a sign of surrender. He looks over at me, but there's something missing in his gaze, a vacancy that I can't and won't put up with.

"Why is she here, Ty?" I ask, but he's already shaking his head.

"I don't know," he admits, tapping some ash into the glass tray next to him. He's shaking a little bit, and I'm not sure if it's the cold or not. Sure, his arms are bare, both sleeves of tattoos gleaming in the stark winter air, but is the icy wind enough to cause goose bumps like that? "Obviously, she's fucked in the head, showing up at our house and all that."

He breathes out a big breath, the warmth clouding in the air like fog.

"She's stalking you then," I say, but Ty is already gazing out across the front yard, towards the rarely traveled road that passes in front of the property, at the trail on the other side that leads to the playground where we made love once.

"Maybe."

"No, not maybe," I say, moving over to stand in front of him, breaking his endless stare. "She *is* stalking you. There's no way her being in town is just a coincidence."

I reach down and grab Ty's cell, gazing at the message and wondering how the fuck she got his number in the first place. I know he never gave it to her, so how? By stalking, that's how. Stupid bitch.

in town. meet @ bar? broken glass i think its called. i know u don't lk me but we have to tlk. Pls reply. Hannah.

And then she has the audacity to put a winky face emoticon. Really? Like, really, bitch? What part about all of this does she think is okay? Raping a thirteen year old boy? Pushing him into the sex trade? Stalking him as a man?

"I don't want her to undo everything we've done," I say, and my voice comes out in a whisper. "Ty, I'm so scared. I don't want her to hurt you. You have enough scars already, more than your fair sure. We have a life now, and I'd rather put a knife through her chest than see her fuck you up with whatever bullshit baggage she brought into town."

Ty stands up suddenly and drops his cigarette by our feet.

He takes my face in his hands and gazes down at me with no small amount of love. There's so much of it that I feel like I'm getting drunk on it. I sway a little on my feet.

He kisses either side of my face with warm lips and then hovers his mouth over mine.

"I don't want you to worry about me, Never. Not like that." He pauses and his mouth twitches. *"I can't go back to yesterday because I was a different person then."*

"Lewis Carroll," I whisper. "You're quoting me *Alice's Adventures in Wonderland*?"

"I know you don't like it when dudes quote shit, but it's kind of fitting, right?"

"I never did like guys quoting poetry. Until you. Ty, I love whatever you do."

I pause and the soft winter silence settles over the two of us.

"If you feel like you need to talk to Hannah, if you … " I feel like my throat is closing up, but I make myself say the words aloud. "If you want to call the police and tell them what you know about Marin Rice, then do it. I know you'll make the right choice. You always do."

He wraps his arms around me then and pulls me close, rests his chin atop my head, and melds our souls into one.

24

I feel like I'm being stabbed with fire pokers, right in the stomach. The sensation freaks me out a little, but the doctor said there was nothing to worry about at my last appointment. I chalk up the sensation to stress. But – and this is fucking huge for me – I will call the stupid ob/gyn tomorrow and ask about it, okay?

"Mini McCabe Number Two doesn't want you to do this," I say, leaning into Ty. This is the thing I like best about using India's truck – there are three seats in the front, so it's kind of ideal for snuggling while driving. Or giving hand jobs. Only Ty still won't let me touch him like that. With the surgery and all, he doesn't think I should be pleasuring him sexually, finds it too weird. I get it. But I wish he'd let me do it anyway.

"Mini McCabe Number Two is a smart little fetus then. I don't even want to do this shit. But I need to. I need this closure." Ty glances over at me with his beautiful brown eyes, like the bark on a really old tree, full of stories and wisdoms and visions past. Brown eyes don't have to be boring eyes. Green leaves might top the trees, and a blue sky might frame them, but without the earth beneath, it would all mean nothing. "And I really, really want her out of my life forever. I don't want to see her again after today, and I'm gonna tell her that. Straight up."

"I love your face," I say and press my lips to his muscular shoulder, one last kiss before we pull into the slanted parking space. The bar brings back even more memories, of slow dancing with Ty, of him punching Luis for me. What a beautiful moment that was.

Ty parks the truck and takes off his seatbelt, glancing up in the rearview mirror for a moment and then pausing like he's been shot. His entire body goes rigid and he sucks in a massive breath.

"Fuck."

I follow his gaze and see Hannah climbing out of her car, honeyed curls swaying in the breeze. She's wearing a baby doll dress in blue, a soft half-smile on her lips. She doesn't even seem to mind the cold, sashaying across the street in a pair of brown booties, a denim jacket slung over one arm. I guess when you have no heart, the cold burn of an icy winter must not be bothersome. Innocuous. Innocuous *poison,* that's what this woman is.

"I feel sick," Ty groans, running his hands down his face. "When I see her, I get all ... twisted up, and I feel like I'm trapped, like I'm never getting out of that hell I was in."

"But you did," I tell him, drawing his hands into my own and running my thumbs across his knuckles. "You did, and this time, you have me by your side."

"You sure you want to go in there?" he asks, leaning close, putting our foreheads together. "You don't have to. You can wait here if you want, read about dirty bikers or rock stars or tattoo artists, whatever the fuck. I just want you and the baby to be safe and happy."

I kiss Ty hard and fierce, hungry, roughly taking his mouth with mine.

It shocks him a little, just enough to snap to him out of the strange mood he's tumbling towards, one that's too empty and dark and lonely for me to bear.

"I'm safest with you, happiest with you, even happier if I get to punch Hannah in the face."

Ty grins at me.

"I could live with that," he says, reaching up to brush a thumb over my lips. "But wait till we get out of the bar before you do it, so nobody sees. You're too hot to go to jail."

"No sane person would lock me up if they knew what Hannah did to you. Besides, I'm pregnant and that earns me a get out of jail free card." I wink at Ty and open the door, smiling even though my words aren't entirely true. I'm sure I would get locked up for beating on this bitch.

She looks so cute and innocent, like a spring fucking flower. And with the way my luck's been going, I'd better not take the chance. Still, if I do get a moment alone with her, I'm not saying it *won't* happen. "Let's get this over with, so we can go home and you can dress our son in that hideous monstrosity of an outfit you ordered."

"Monstrosity? That's a flying purple people eater costume."

I raise my brows at him before climbing out, glad that for a second here, we can infuse the air with laughter, with smiles. I know it won't last long once we get in there.

"Exactly. That's what I said: monstrosity."

I glance around but don't see Hannah anywhere. Good. I take a moment to compose myself as Ty steps up beside me, perfectly beautiful in a pair of old jeans, a yellow SOG tee, and his customary pair of boots. I have his jacket wrapped around me, his baby inside of me, and a killer purple dress (also stolen from India). I had to look good for this, better than Hannah, but not for Ty – for myself.

"Last time," Ty whispers, reaching down to take my hand. "Last time either of us will ever have to put up with her or her shit." He steels himself, shoulders back, jaw locked tight, and then he moves us forward and into the doors of the Broken Glass, into a world of useless drunks, lonely souls, and wide-eyed drifters.

Hannah is at the bar, already surrounded by men. She has several drinks lined up in front of her and a smile on her face.

I wish a lighting bolt would shoot down from the sky, crack the roof, and turn her head into burnt pudding. If she died right now, I wouldn't feel a scrap of remorse or shed a single tear. If that makes me a bad person, then so be it. I have no sympathy for people like her.

"Tyson," she says, but Ty doesn't cringe when she uses his name. In fact, he barely acknowledges her, finding us an empty table and pulling my chair out for me. After a quick look around, I'm relieved to see that tonight, Luis isn't at his usual watering hole. *Thank God.* I don't think I could deal with two demons all in one night.

Ty sits down beside me, close enough that our legs touch, and then crosses his arms over his chest to wait. Hannah's eyes alight on me as if she's just seeing me for the first time. When she makes her way over to the table, a drink in either hand, I can tell she's not happy to see me here. Too fucking bad for her.

"The bartender is skilled for a man who works in the middle of nowhere."

Ty puts his hands flat on the table as Hannah sets a drink in front of him. When he looks at her, his expression is completely blank, as if she's not worthy of emotion. I like that. He really is cutting her off, snipping away the bad memories, letting them drown in a sea of darkness to be forgotten.

"We're not here to chat with you, Hannah," Ty says, pushing the drink back towards her. "And my wife is pregnant, so neither of us will be drinking either." I see the flash on Hannah's face when Ty says those key words. *Wife. Pregnant.* She's jealous of me, whether she wants to admit it or not.

"Then why did you come?" she asks, sitting down, tucking her skirt beneath her legs with a gracefulness that bothers the hell out of me. Like with my mother, I wish Hannah's outside would match her inside. If it did, she'd be a withered crone with melted lips and sightless eyes, pus swollen fingers, and an empty chest cavity where her heart should be. Too bad the world doesn't work like that.

"How did you get my number, Hannah? How the fuck did you find me?" Ty leans forward, his dark hair gleaming beneath the dull lights of the bar. It's beautiful, even in here. And he looks so badass with his silver piercings, his tattoos, the way his jaw tightens as he looks at her. Barely coiled violence curls under his skin, but that's okay. He's holding it back, and that's where his true strength lies.

"I have my ways," she says, unfolding and refolding the red paper napkin under her drink. When she looks up, her eyes flicker between blue and green, like the ocean on a hot summer day. They shouldn't look like that, the eyes of a predator. They should be yellow and slitted with two sets of eyelids instead of long curling lashes. "I told you before, Tyson, that all kinds of information gets passed around in my circle. When the cops came looking for information about Marin, after her family put up the reward money, your name started being tossed around. I'm not the only one that knows where you live."

Hannah picks up her drink and sips it from the tiny red straw, all dainty and shit. It takes everything I have inside of me to sit still.

"Is that a threat?" I growl, but Hannah refuses to acknowledge my presence, still staring at my husband as if she could get him to crack. He won't. Nothing she says tonight will matter to him.

"Answer my wife's question," he says, and I notice her fingers tighten almost imperceptibly around the dew covered glass in her hand. Ty sits back and crosses his arms over his chest again.

"I'm not threatening you, Tyson. All I'm doing is telling you the truth. I came here to ask you to let bygones be bygones. What happened to Marin was terrible, but it wasn't your fault." Hannah leans over and tries to touch Ty's arm, but he pulls away. "It wasn't my fault either. You do know that, right?" Ty continues to say nothing, and I watch as Hannah struggles to come up with a convincing argument. "You can tell them about Marin, but you're only implicating yourself."

"Maybe the truth deserves to be out there, don't you think?" he asks, voice quietly menacing, as if the word *truth* is a sword that he could stab right through Hannah's throat. "Marin deserves justice, doesn't she?"

"Justice," Hannah says as she sets her drink down on the table and rises to her feet. "Means all kinds of different things to different people." She pauses and looks between Ty and me for a moment before picking up her jacket. "I wish you good luck with yours."

25

As soon as Hannah exits the bar, Ty is grabbing my hand and pulling me up.

"What are you doing?" I ask as he tugs me towards the door. The look on his face when he glances back at me is terrifying.

"Something's up with her. Remember my fucktard-dar? It's going off like fucking crazy right now. Come on." Ty takes me outside and opens the passenger side door of the truck, glancing surreptitiously over his shoulder at Hannah. In the rearview mirror I watch her, too, watch her smoking a cigarette, pulling out her cell for a quick text. Whatever clue she gave Ty that she was up to something, I'm not seeing, but I trust him anyway. If Ty says the bitch is full of shit, then I believe it as surely as if I saw her do something with my own eyes.

Ty closes my door and moves over to the driver's side, climbing in and starting the engine. He even pulls out of the space and drives around the block, turning us down a side street and parking in the shadows beneath the old bank building.

Hannah is still standing by her car, talking on her cell phone, but after a few moments, she gets in and takes off, too.

"You're not seriously going to try and follow her?" I ask, but Ty just smiles tightly and puts his foot on the gas, turning the corner and following a discreet distance behind Hannah's black sedan. Fancy, expensive. It's nice, too nice for someone like her, nicer even than the red one she showed up in at our house in New York. I wonder how she makes her money, if she gets it all from sex trafficking, selling off boys like Ty to men without souls.

"We're like spies or some shit," McCabe says, trying his best to lighten the mood. It works, at least a little anyway. "First we tracked Luis, now this? Pretty cool, right? Maybe I could get a job as a professional sleuth or something?"

"Because you're so inconspicuous?" I ask, reaching over and poking Ty right in a purple butterfly tattoo. He smiles, but his dimples have definitely left the building.

He's trying to joke, trying to be strong, but I know even a brief encounter with a demon can set someone back. I squeeze his bicep and press our bodies together, loving the way his right hand immediately drops off the wheel and curls around my knee. We were made to be mates, Ty and me. We work best as a unit.

"Thanks for coming with me. I know it can't have been easy for you either."

"However hard it was for me, it was ten times that for you. At least it was over before it really started." I pause and glance up into his face. "Are you feeling okay?" Ty nods, and even though I know I wouldn't be alright after a tense encounter with my rapist, I believe him. He's strong in so many ways, too many to count. After all, strength in the face of luxury and ease isn't truly strength at all; strength against all the odds, against pain and heartache and poverty and loss, that's the good stuff right there.

"At this point, I'm just hoping my hunch is all for nothing, that I'm imagining shit, you know?"

"And what kind of hunch do you have exactly?"

Ty plays with his lip ring for a moment before answering.

"She came all the way down here for a five second conversation? I'm just not buying it."

"Maybe I scared her off?" I joke, but Ty's tight smile says he's still worried. Then again, maybe he's right to worry? She did stalk him like a crazy person, toss out a veiled threat, and then leave without hardly saying anything at all.

I sit back and try to calm the sudden queasiness in my belly. Maybe Mini McCabe has a hunch, too? *Please let this all turn out okay. I don't think I can handle anymore tragic situations or broken hearts, loss or that devastating sense of what-if.* Fuck.

At least I don't have to sit with my anxiety for long; it takes just a few minutes of driving in the dark, straight out of town and towards the lake I went to that first night with Noah. Ty goes right past the exit at first, letting Hannah turn onto the quiet road leading towards the campground area. As cold as it is right now, and with the freak little flurries of snow we've been getting, I doubt there's anyone else there.

I start to get nervous.

Unused campgrounds, middle of the night, middle of nowhere, that's where bad shit happens. I know. I've been around plenty of it. Ty, too.

"Why'd you drive past?" I ask him, but he's already flipping a bitch and heading back in the other direction. I watch him play with his lip ring again, left hand tightening on the steering wheel.

"I didn't want to spook her," is all he says before he shuts off the headlights and turns down the campground road, past a few lonely RVs, and straight to the mostly empty campsites.

There's only one that has a car parked in it, and that's where Ty stops, blocking Hannah in with the truck. Before I can even ask if there's a plan, he's climbing out and taking off after her.

I stumble after him, hitting the dirt road with a sudden burst of dizziness. *Fuck.* I hate being pregnant. Why can't I be a glowing maternity ad with shining hair and a beatific smile? Shit.

I look across the campsite and see Ty standing

beneath the swags of old fashioned Edison bulbs, draped between the trees, like our little homestead is the epitome of Old Town Midwest America. Even in the off-season, it looks picture perfect.

Ty is panting, chest heaving with big breaths, and his hands are curled into fists by his sides. It takes me another minute or two to spot Hannah, halfway out of the fancy black foreign whatever-the-fuck-it-is car.

"Tyson," she says, and I can see the way Ty's body reacts to her, like he's been poisoned and simultaneously slapped in the face, kicked in the nuts, and run over by a car. He shudders and goose bumps crawl all over his skin. "What are you doing here?"

"The fuck is this?" he asks, and his voice is barely coherent, half anger and all pain. "What is this, Hannah?" His tone is rising sharply, careening into the realm of panic. I look both ways before climbing out of the pickup – these country fucks drive crazy and I refuse to lose another baby because I'm not paying attention.

When it's clear, I jog over to stand next to Ty.

Hannah is not happy to see me, tucking some of her honeyed curls behind an ear as she climbs out, booted heels loud on the hard packed earth beneath our feet.

"Now let me explain," she begins, but Ty is beyond listening to her. He storms forward like a thunder cloud, rolling in dark and deadly. His combat boots get up and personal with Hannah's shoes and his eyes flash with a thousand shades of darkness that my soul recognizes all too well.

"Open the fucking door," he says softly. His voice is scary now, different than I've ever heard before. I can't stop staring at him, can't quite figure out what's going on.

And then I hear a familiar voice from the backseat.

"Can we roast marshmallows now?"

Darla.

This bitch has Darla.

I lunge forward and grab the handle, but it's locked. I yank and pull anyway, kick the side of the sleek black piece of shit before spinning to face her. If I was mad before, I'm not even really sure what I am now.

"Open the fucking door!" I scream, and I don't care that my voice is echoing around the campground – hell, maybe the ranger will show up to see what this scuffle is all about. "NOW." It's not a suggestion.

"Just let me explain, okay?" Hannah says, her weird green-blue eyes too pale in her face, like some sort of husky dog gone wrong. "Hear me out."

"Did you touch my sister?" I ask, voice like ice, slithering from my lips like a snake. If looks, words, if they could kill, mine would be doing exactly that now, sinking their teeth into this bitch's throat and injecting enough venom to drop an elephant.

"No!" Hannah looks around like she's afraid someone might overhear. Guess what? I give zero fucks about that. I reach out and shove her forward, *hard.* She stumbles, but not for long enough, grabbing onto the car door to stay upright. "Listen to me!" Hannah is screaming, but I don't care what she has to say. There aren't words to explain away what she's done. She can tell her story to the cops.

"Careful, Never," Ty says, grabbing my upper arm, making me look at him. "She isn't worth it. She's not."

I stare at him, and I know he's right. Right now, my only mission is to get Darla and call the cops. That's it.

Our current justice system doesn't allow for me to put a knife to this woman's throat – although I'd like to. Oh God, I'd like to.

"Back the fuck up, Hannah," Ty says, releasing my arm and shouldering past her. She stumbles away and comes around behind him, her eyes narrowed on me, hands shaking. She looks so innocent in her blue baby doll dress, almost pretty. Just more proof that monsters come in all shapes and sizes. Never judge a book by its cover has never seemed so accurate. A beautiful demon is still a demon, and I won't let her hurt my family anymore.

Ty unlocks the doors and in a one, short beautiful second, Darla is in his arms. She looks okay, a little confused maybe, but happy to see us. I don't see any visible bruises or cuts, but I know best that sometimes the worst scars run deepest. God help Hannah if she touched my little sister like she did Ty. Then, then not even the threat of jail will keep me from putting her six feet under, I swear it.

"Are you okay, honey?" I ask, brushing back her hair, feeling tears prick my eyes. *She's okay. I can't believe she's okay. But why? Why take Darla? And how? How did this bitch even get a hold of her in the first place?*

"Hannah, um, Hannah said we could do marshmallows," Darla says, twisting her hands in Ty's black T-shirt. I press my cheek to hers, say a quick prayer of thanks to the universe, and pull out my cell to call the cops. And then Beth. Oh God, Beth.

"Please wait," Hannah says as I turn to look at her. "Let me explain things before you call the police."

"You're so lucky I'm holding a baby right now," Ty

says, voice cold and dark. "Maybe we both are? I wouldn't want to go to prison for you."

I start dialing the cops when Hannah reaches out and snatches my wrist, makes me drop the phone. Ty immediately goes to set Darla down and come to my rescue, but he should know better. I know how to take care of myself. I hit Hannah right in her piggy little nose with the heel of my hand and feel a sharp crack in response. She takes a defensive swing at my face and misses, giving me the chance to step in and grab a handful of her perfect fucking hair and shove her to her knees where she belongs. A quick punch up hits me right in the stomach and I feel my entire body go numb.

"Never!"

Ty is pulling me back, catching me in his arms as I wilt, like a flower with too little water and too much sun, but Hannah is already standing up and taking off down the road like the rogue fugitive little bitch that she is.

"Get her, Ty!" I screech, but he won't let go of me, swinging me up into his arms like I weigh nothing. "Ty, get her!" I yell, hitting him in the chest while pain flashes white behind my eyelids. In that moment, I'm mad at him for not taking off, beating the shit out of Hannah. Later, I'll realize that his restraint is his true strength.

He sets me down on the hood of Hannah's car and my mind flashes back to that day so long ago outside the convenience store, when he picked me up out of that broken glass like a true prince.

Ty brackets my face between his hands, looking into my eyes with a bead of sweat clinging to the tip of his nose. I've scared the crap out of him – again.

"Baby, are you okay?"

I have my arms wrapped around my body like a coat, struggling against the sudden rush of nausea.

"I'm fine. Call the police."

"I'm calling a fucking ambulance," he says, bending down to grab my phone and put an arm around Darla. Ty lifts her up and holds her tight while he dials, leaning his forehead against mine. "You are so strong and so stubborn and so perfect, but fuck. You're going to give me a heart attack one of these days."

I smile, even through the pain.

If the blood on my hand is any indication, Hannah got at least a little bit of the karma that's due her. And we have Darla back, seemingly whole and unscathed.

If I had sneakers with me, I'd put them on because, maybe, just maybe, it might be time for me to start climbing out of this valley.

26

I have never seen a reunion like the one that happens on our front porch, a burst of life and love and brightness, relief and even a little bit of fear. Beth is so relieved that Darla is still alive that she collapses to her knees at the foot of the steps, falls to the icy ground in nothing but a peach colored shift, her copper tangle of hair twisted on her head like a nest. She doesn't look disheveled in that moment though, just beautiful, like an ancient earth goddess come home to rest.

Darla seems a little confused, unsure as to why everyone is so excited to see her but happy nonetheless. Well, for the first five minutes or so she's happy and then she just seems done with the whole hugging and kissing and crying thing. Then she goes right back to asking for toasted marshmallows. Makes me wonder exactly what Hannah told her.

"You're okay?" Beth asks after the police have gone and the house seems almost ... normal again. I know that's not true, that my mother's absence although not immediately obvious will undoubtedly leave some sort of scar. "The baby?"

She licks her lips and straightens her shoulders, regaining some of that essential Beth-ness that has been missing along with Darla.

"We're fine," I say, because we are. The doctor even said so. Mini McCabe Two is still only a cluster of cells and already she can take a punch. Yup, this is definitely Ty's kid. "You?"

"I'm concerned," Beth says, but I can see her relief is so great it's hard to focus on any of that right now. Darla's return has swept even my mother's death from her mind. At least for the moment anyway. "But I'm glad, glad that Darla is back, glad that woman got caught. So glad." She tears up again and turns away, waving me off when I try to step closer to her. "I'm fine. Really." Beth sniffles a little and glances back over at us, at Ty McCabe whose face is tilted up to the stars.

I don't like his expression; it's too far away.

"Give us a minute," I tell her and we exchange a soft smile, packed with more words and emotions than anyone could ever understand – not unless they have a sister, too.

"Sure thing, hon. Just don't stay out here too long. You'll catch your death." Beth squeezes my shoulder and turns away, moving up the steps and into the house. The moment feels so hush-hush, like the world is just waiting to breathe. It's a trick of the winter wind and the cold, the gentle cloud cover that mutes the stars.

I step over to the love of my life, my very own bad boy, and I curl myself around his arm. Ty starts like he didn't even know I was there and smiles softly. No dimples though, damn it.

"This isn't your fault," I say and his breath catches sharply. I keep going before he can fill the air with profane words of wisdom, cloud my mind from what I need to say. "You heard the cops. My mom dropped Darla off here and left her. She left a fucking *four year old* alone with Netflix and a bowl of microwave popcorn. If she hadn't done that, Hannah never would've had a chance to pick her up. Besides, they fucking arrested her bitch ass, so who cares?" I poke Ty in the chest, but he doesn't budge.

"Hannah is only here because of me," Ty whispers, breath fogging in the cool air. He keeps his gaze on the stars and won't look at me. "She's only in your life, your family's life, your son's life because I fucked up once upon a time." He drops his eyes down to mine and I see that shimmer of blackness there that delves right down into his soul, into his horrible past, a past that's ten times worse than mine. A hundred. A thousand. "I let her hit you. I failed you, Never, as a man."

I snort and reach up to tug on Ty's nose ring.

"Are you kidding me? The measure of a man isn't if he can throw the first punch. It's in how well he supports his woman when she does." Ty's mouth twitches, but there are still no dimples. "A real man loves like there's no tomorrow, cares for his kids as if there's always one, and kisses like yesterday never happened."

A soft chuckles escapes his throat as he turns to me, putting his hands on either side of my waist.

"You made that up just now, didn't you?"

I quirk a brow at him.

"Of course I did. Can't you tell it doesn't make any real sense?"

"It makes perfect sense," Ty says, moving his ringed fingers to my chin and tilting my face up. "Because you said it. Everything you say makes sense to me." He leans in like he's going to kiss me and then just stops. "But I still wish I would've backhanded the bitch."

"You punched Luis for me, remember? So we're even. You took out my past; I gave a smack down to yours."

Ty wrinkles his brow for a moment and then nods.

"I suppose I can live with that."

And then he really does kiss me like yesterday never happened, like this is our first kiss all over again. I feel the same butterflies in my belly, the fireworks behind my eyelids, the fire in my veins.

I kiss him and I know that this is what a soul mate tastes like.

27

"I've never seen so many nude photos in one place," Ty says with a slight wrinkle of his nose. He sets aside another stack of pictures, nestling them carefully into a shoe box marked *Not For Human Consumption*. I wrote that as a joke and then felt guilty afterward. Thing is, I don't know how to feel about finding naked photos of my dead mother. It's weird and awful in so many ways. "Only place that rivals this porn palace is the Internet."

I give a sad smile and shuffle through some more shots of my mother dancing. Sitting here, doing this, it's hard but I know I have to do it. Beth had to take Darla to a psychologist, one that specializes in child abuse, to attempt to get the full story and determine if Hannah did anything inappropriate to her. Apparently we're all going to have to go in at some point and give interviews. Fine by me. I've already had a few with the police anyway – we all have. Well, except for Ty. He made an appointment with one of the detectives to go down tomorrow and give a statement. I know that in this statement, he's going to tell them everything. Everything. He's going to implicate himself and although his only sin is that he ran away, kept his mouth shut all these years, I'm still scared. I don't know shit about the justice system or how any of that works. Is Ty an accessory to murder?

I take a shuddering breath and watch as his face lifts to mine.

"There are so many pictures of Angelica in here," I say, dropping my pile to my lap and rubbing my temples with fingernails dipped in black. I painted them for her. It was all I could do really. I can't make myself cry for her anymore, miss her, care that she's gone. It sounds horrible, I know, and I don't want to be a horrible, numb useless sort of person. I *want* to weep like Jade, to be like India and cry when nobody's looking. Now that Darla's back, it's finally started to settle on the house that my mother is really and truly gone. The fear for our sister, the overwhelming emotions we had for her, they've settled back down like a dust cloud and now, now we can see my mother's metaphorical casket, shining black and lined with roses.

Only, I'm not missing her, not sad for her, only for the idea of what should've been. I'm mourning a caricature of a person that I've drawn up inside my head, an ideal of what a mother should be.

"She has pictures of herself laughing and dancing and drinking and fucking." I sigh and drag another box over towards my knee. Chuck Norris lounges on the bed, his eyes narrowing on me like he knows something I don't. He's a brave cat, really, the only person that will dare to sleep on that bed. Even Jade, missing our momma like there's no tomorrow, she won't come in here and touch it. "There are no pictures of her kids in here." I pause and feel my mouth tighten. "No pictures of *us*. There are no pictures of her lovers or even that yellow lab she had all those years ago. Pretty sure she loved her more than me and yet, there are no pictures of the fucking dog."

Ty scoots closer and bumps his knee into mine. The motion soothes some of my ire, just enough that I can think clearly.

"At least your mom had pictures of you," I say, "and she didn't throw away a single thing that used to be yours." Ty leans into me and sighs.

"Nor did she throw away all those bottles of her own piss. Besides, your mom left your room locked up like a museum. If we're exchanging fucked up mommy stories, I think you'll find us tied for first." Ty curls his left hand around mine, bandage still firmly in place. I wonder if his burn will leave a scar and decide that I don't care either way – Ty and I are already scarred and we're all the more beautiful for it. "I think in her own way, she really did love you." I snort, but Ty shushes me by turning and placing his lips against my ear. "You're pretty easy to love, you know, even for someone like her."

I ignore his words because I'm not sure how comfortable I am with them. Maybe, by believing she didn't love me at all, it's easier for me to let her go?

I reach into the box at my left and pull out some crumpled papers. Past due bills abound, mixed in with receipts galore, a few shopping lists. What I want to find, but that I doubt I ever will, is some proof, some answer to the whole Luis story. Why did he kill Dad? And why, why did she marry him? I hate thinking that I might have to live the rest of my life not knowing. I want this story wrapped up in a perfect, little bow. I want to know, want to shelve it, want to forget about it.

But life doesn't usually offer up those sorts of things, does it? It's ambiguous at best, an enigma at worst.

"Hey," Ty says, just as I'm about to mark the entire box for the burn pile. "What's this?"

He leans over me and shoves some of the crap aside, retrieving a small, colorful sheet of paper in his ringed hand. On second look, it's actually a napkin, crinkled and old, stained with a bit of something that looks like coffee. My husband hands it to me with a raised brow, asking without words if I know what this is.

The strangest thing is, I do.

There's a picture on the napkin, a few garbled stick figures drawn in thick crayon. Me, Beth, Zella, Jade, Dad, Mom. In her flowery, loose handed writing style, Angelica has written the names of each person above their lopsided heads.

"Hey you," my momma says as she sips her coffee and reaches out to ruffle my hair. She was supposed to

come home last night and read me a story, but she didn't. Papa says Momma gets confused sometimes and forgets how much she likes being with her family. "You okay?"

I nod and fidget in my seat. I like comin' to the cafe because it smells good and the lady behind the counter always gives me a chocolate chip cookie when her boss isn't lookin'. But I am a little bored. I wish I had one of those fancy video game systems like Noah's got.

Momma looks over at me, her curls piled up on her head, her neck decorated with a necklace draped in silver coins.

"Here," she says, reaching into her purse and grabbing a box of crayons. I take them from her fingers and open the lid carefully, like I ain't never had a present from anybody before. Momma rarely gives presents and she rarely takes us kids anywhere. But I'm here now, with her, just the two of us.

The crayons are half-broke and there's no yellow, but I don't care. I'm too happy to care.

I smile up at her, beaming like an angel – until I realize there's no paper.

I frown and open my mouth to speak, but Momma's already got that part covered.

"Use this," she says, pushing her napkin over to my side of the table. "Draw me the thing you love most in the world, and I'll get you a hot cocoa."

I grin excitedly and start to draw. I'm good at assignments – teacher even said so at the last report card meetin' – but since Momma wasn't there, I'll have to prove it to her now. Besides, this is a real easy one for me. I know exactly what to draw without even having to think twice about it.

Momma goes to stand up and then pauses, glancing over at me with a weird lookin' expression on her face. I glance up at her, and she softens her face into a smile.

"I love you, baby girl, even if I'm no good at showing it."

"Never?" Ty's voice wakes me from the memory at the same moment his thumb brushes across my cheek, coming away wet and glistening. His beautiful lips curve into the most perfect smile. "See," he says, dropping his voice to a suggestive whisper. "Even when you think all hope's gone out the window, it always finds a way to come back."

"Like a butterfly," I say, sniffling and letting the tears fall like raindrops.

"Exactly like a butterfly."

28

Darla is not just home, but she's safe. She has no injuries, physical ones anyway. As far as her mental state goes, she's exactly like normal, too young to comprehend our mother's death and too detached from the woman to even notice she's missing. See, one of grief's worst attributes is that it likes to cling to the everyday, remind you how different life is. A person who was always there, a smiling face that always held a grin, the bright ring of laughter, if it's always around then you notice when it's missing. But if it's not? Imagine getting rid of your favorite shirt, your go-to, something you wore on a regular basis. Now imagine climbing into the basement or the attic or a spare bedroom and getting rid of some random thing that's been stored in there. Sure, it might mean something to you, might even be an heirloom or something, but you didn't see it everyday and so you can't miss it everyday.

That's Angelica.

I'd probably miss my dog more if she passed away. Which she's going to if she can't stop licking my fucking feet. I block bitch-Angelica's tongue with my hand and listen intently to what Beth is saying about the psychologist that Darla went to see.

"She says she's as confident as she can be that nothing happened while Hannah had Darla. Apparently they camped out a few nights at the park and roasted marshmallows or something." Beth sighs and tucks some hair behind her ears. "Anyway, she said that these sorts of situations are never black and white, cut and dry, but that she'd bet her career on her observations. Darla is okay," Beth says this last part with a sudden smile. "I trust her, too. I mean, you should see the big fancy office she has in Jackson. It's a part of her house, but it's still nicer than anything around here." My sister gets out one of her nasty ass menthol cigarettes and rises to her feet.

Ty is sitting next to me, but he's barely there, one booted foot tapping out a rhythm on the floor.

Today he has his appointment with the detective. I'm both scared and strangely excited. Scared because I don't know what could happen and excited because I know what will. No matter what the outcome, Ty will have this bit of his past shoved off his shoulders and into somebody else's hands. He can finally make things right, turn that guilt into something better.

I reach down and squeeze his hand and he starts like I've just splashed his face with cold water.

"That's fucking fantastic, Beth," he says and I know he means it. I think Ty loves my sisters as much as I do. And I love him for that.

"You'll do great, Ty," she says, coming over to pet his hair with a motherly sort of affection. "And when you get back, I'll have dinner waiting on the table. Who wants pot roast?" Beth raises the hand with the cigarette in it and smiles, but I'm already gagging. Hello morning sickness, thanks for coming back to punch me in the gut. Maybe I should get my tubes tied when I have this kid? I don't think Ty and I will ever fully accept condoms. There's just something so stimulating about having his bare flesh inside of mine. Of course, there's always the pill and whatnot, but those aren't a hundred percent effective and Ty is so fertile that I need as close to that as I can get. "I'm going outside for a smoke," Beth tells us and disappears through the screen door.

Ty and I sit in silence for a while, just holding hands, absorbing each other. I have a colored napkin tucked in my back pocket and some of my mother's bracelets on my arm. I feel so much better now than I have in weeks, since her death, since Darla's disappearance. Grief still nibbles at my guilty soul, but that's okay. I can deal with this.

"Whatever happens today, I love you more than I could ever say in words." Ty turns to look at me, fully and completely serious. His piercings are absent, leaving little holes where they're supposed to go. I know he's trying to look professional for the meeting, but I hope he puts them back in as soon as he's done. I like Ty just the way he is. "And I'm sorry," he whispers again.

I shake my head.

"Stop doing that. Stop apologizing for everything. None of this is your fault." He still blames himself for the pregnancy, for my almost dying, for Darla's kidnapping. I can't bear it.

"I'm going to make things right. I don't care what rules I break or who I piss off. I *have* to tell the truth now. I'm going to rat out every person I ever met when I was involved in all of that shit, every client, every dirty deed. If one boy, just one, gets spared what I went through because I speak up, then it'll all be worth it."

I lean in and kiss Ty's lips softly, just enough for him to taste my feelings on the breath that passes between us.

"You're going to do fine, Ty. You always do."

He nods and stands up, drawing me with him.

"Think I should wear slacks and loafers?" he asks as the front door opens up and Beth reappears, her face flustered and her mouth quivering. Ten seconds after, there he is, Danny the Asshat Delphino.

"*Fuuuuck,*" Ty drawls, sagging just a bit. "We're due for a day without douche bags, aren't we?"

Danny pauses and glances over at Ty with disdain dripping from the sharp frown that's cut into his face like a scar. *He* is wearing slacks and loafers.

"No slacks and loafers," I tell Ty, giving Danny a look. "I've suddenly developed a bad taste in my mouth for them."

"I have parental rights," he tells Beth, deciding to ignore me and Ty. Smart move on his part. "You've kept my daughters from me for weeks, and now that your little crisis is over, I want them back."

"You can't just drop in here unannounced whenever you damn well feel like it, Danny." Beth turns around, rubbing at her nose with the back of one hand. I hate how undone she becomes in this man's presence. Truly, it scares the crap out of me. "We're a whole family again. I need this now. My mother just passed away, and I want my girls by my side. By Darla's side." I don't miss the whole family comment, how my mother really was never a part of it.

"And I have some functions in Jackson that I'd like to take my daughters to."

"Autumn is an infant and Maple is three. What sort of functions could you possibly be taking them to?"

"My fiancée is in town and she'd like to meet the kids," Danny says and I can visibly see Beth sway from the news. Fuck. Did he come over here just to hurt her like that? Drive the nail of grief a little deeper? I clench my fists at my sides and do my best not to get involved.

"What if I just say no?" Beth says, standing up tall and getting in Danny's face. She plays with his tie for a moment before letting go and putting some space between them.

"Then I'll just have to call the police and let them know my parental rights are being obstructed." Beth turns away, the white and pink dress she's wearing swaying with the motion. She tilts her chin down like she's thinking really, really hard about something. I guess that whatever it is, it's not worth the fight. She breathes in deep and then looks back at Danny.

"Fine."

That's it, just that one word so heavy with defeat that I feel like *I'm* drowning, even though I'm not directly involved.

"Fine?" Ty asks, drawing Danny's sharp gaze over to him. Now that we're living here, I know we're going to see a whole lot more of these visits. Each and every time I'm going to get angry, going to wonder why a father who uses his kids as little more than accessories to please his new fiancée, should get to pull them away from their mother when she needs them the most.

Thing is, the world isn't fair, won't ever be fair. I'm wholly and completely aware of that. Doesn't make it any easier to watch. I curl my hand around Ty's bicep as a warning. He's on edge because of the meeting; I get that. But I won't let him jeopardize himself for something that isn't worth it – just like he did for me. Danny hardly has a passing interest in his daughters. These little visits are all part of some freak power struggle that he thinks he needs to have with Beth. I can see from his beady little stare that he can't stand the idea that she turned him down.

"Let it go," I tell Ty and he nods like he's actually going to listen to me.

"I'll get their things," Beth says, moving up the stairs like a zombie, hand curled so tightly around the bannister that her skin looks paper thin, like her bones could pop out at any moment. As soon as she's out of sight, Ty steps close to Danny.

"Honestly, I'm kind of glad you're taking them." He clears his throat. "Maple has these little red dots all over her arm. I'm thinking chicken pox. Autumn'll probably catch 'em, too."

Danny bristles, but he doesn't bat an eyelash.

"Do you think I'm stupid?" he asks instead, and Ty pauses like he's thinking really hard about that question.

"Not if you're vaccinated," is all he decides to say and then moves back over to me, taking my hand and pulling me into the kitchen for a moment. We busy ourselves pretending to make toast and then exchange a look when we hear the sound of the screen door slamming shut.

When Beth comes back downstairs, she finds me sitting as close as I can get to my dark soul mate, munching peanut butter toast from our spot on the window seat. She raises a brow at us.

"Where the fuck did Danny go?"

29

I wait outside the police station in Beth's minivan, engine still running, heater blasting my face as I play with my new eReader and try to decide what to read. After fucking around with it for a good thirty minutes, I shove it back in my purse with a scowl.

It's always a bad sign when reading, the most entrancing of all escapes, isn't enough. I am so *desperate* to not be here right now, that I can't get away. My anxiety levels are off the charts and my stomach is turning somersaults. Now I can see why Ty wanted me to wait at home. With all of this stress, I'm liable to open the damn door and vomit all over the police parking lot. Bet they'd like that, wouldn't they?

I take a deep breath and lean my head back against the seat. This is not their fault. The cops are the good guys here. I just have to keep telling myself that. No matter what they do to Ty, they're the good guys. What happened to Marin Rice was horrible beyond belief, raped and murdered, dumped, no sign of justice anywhere. If Ty can simultaneously implicate Hannah and the rest of her fucked up gang of sex trade buddies, then the world will be all the better for it. Even if Ty suffers, too.

I moan because the pain is so raw, so emotional that it's become physical. I don't want Ty to suffer. I lied. I'm a selfish person. I'd rather he was at home safe with me than here doing the right thing. I know that's a terrible thing to think, but I don't give a shit.

I turn off the engine because the heat feels suddenly stifling and force myself to move from the passenger seat into the back row. The center row is literally filled with carseats, so this is the only place I can go to lay down and not be seen; the windows are tinted back here thankfully.

I lay on my side for a while, a long time. I have no idea how long because I'm hurting so bad and worrying so hard, and then eventually I just fall into a fitful slumber.

I dream of my mother, and my father's death, of myself dancing on a stage with only the two of them in the audience. As I'm spinning and twirling, swaying with the music, I hear a sound, like the jangling of bells. It draws my attention like no other, wakes me up inside in the most brilliant sort of way.

"Baby, you awake?"

It's Ty, shaking my shoulder gently, turning me to face him. The first thing I see when I open my eyes is how red rimmed and sad his are. I can't take it, so I sit up suddenly and throw my arms around his neck, holding him, just holding him as tight as I possibly can. Outside the sky is starting to get dark, so I know we've been here for quite some time.

"I came out a few hours ago to see you, but you were already fast asleep. I thought about calling Beth to come and get you, but I'm a selfish man, Nev. I wanted you here with me, even though I wished you weren't, when you should've been at home relaxing and drinking hot chocolate. I'm sorry, baby. So sorry."

He's crying, but not for me, for himself. For the boy he was. For the cousin he lost. For the mother who should've protected and loved him as fiercely as I do, as fiercely as I'll protect and love our own son.

"It's okay, it's okay," I whisper, letting him bury his face in my shoulder and squeeze me tight.

"Sorry to be such a wuss," he whispers with a small chuckle, trying to play off his emotions as nothing. But see, even if he was crying over a stubbed toe (not that he would because even though he's a sweetie, let's be honest, he's still a tough as nails, melt the panties badass), I would care. I would care because he's everything to me, so all that he feels, I feel. I feel it times ten, and I'd do anything to absorb it and take it away from him, cure him with my love. It's okay because I know I could do that, because Ty is right. Love is not a pie to be sliced and handed out until it's gone; love is an endless well. Even if you think it's run dry, if you search long and hard enough, you'll always find another cool drink. "Told you guys were pussies."

"If you're trying to say men are weak, then I'd use the term *balls*. Balls are weak. Pussies can expand and shove out squalling babies." Ty snorts, and I know I've made the right choice. Joke, laugh, smile. I used to think those were just cover-ups for bad feelings, that if you did that, they'd come and resurface at the most inopportune moments possible. While I think that might be true in some cases, I now know that it's okay to grin and giggle in a tough situation. Life is short. That grin or giggle could be your very last, and I don't know about you, but I'd rather go out in a burst of laughter than a spray of tears.

"True that. Trust me, I've *seen* it," he says with a pretend shudder.

"Well, I've lived it," I say, leaning back to press a kiss to Ty's forehead. He can act like he was all grossed out and whatever at Noah's birth, but I saw the slight sheen of tears in his eyes then, just like I do now. "What happened in there?"

Ty takes a deep breath and sits back, wedging his body into that awkward space between the center seat and the sliding door. He folds his hands around his knees and looks straight at me.

"I relived it all. From start to finish, I told the whole story. Everything. And it hurt like hell, Never. It fucking *burned*," Ty touches a hand to his chest and the bracelets on his arms jingle, "but it also felt good. Now they know everything I know, and I feel like some of the burden is off of me." Ty licks his lips and glances to the side as I crawl off the seat and come over to him, nestling myself between his legs and letting him cradle my head on his lap. I close my eyes and listen to his voice, knowing that sound could lull me to sleep any day, could lull me to sleep for forever. "They want me to testify. Against Hannah. Against ... they've got two people in custody for the murder of Marin Rice, Never. They fit my description, and they want me to testify." He goes quiet for a moment and I don't say anything because I know he needs to puzzle through this on his own first. "I told them I wouldn't do anything that might put my family in danger. Hannah might be a punk and a freak, but she's telling the truth. Prostitution isn't all *Pretty Woman* and shit. There are gangs ... fuck, there are *mafia* groups, cartels that deal in this shit, in sex trafficking." Ty pauses and strokes his fingers through my hair. I wonder if he's thinking the same thing I am: he's lucky. Ty is so lucky. He escaped, he survived, he has a chance to thrive. Not everyone gets that chance. "I was never high enough up in the ranking to know anything about anything, so this could be nothing ... but it could be everything, too."

"I'm not afraid," I tell Ty because I'm not. To me, his sanity is worth everything, his conscious, his heart. Plus, I've seen him punch out a dude with a fistful of rings. Ty is outwardly calm, and he loves like a fucking beast, but I know this darkness we both have, it knows how to fight back, how to protect itself. I don't think there's much this world could throw at us that we couldn't take – especially together.

There's a long pause, and I decide to sit up, looking at Ty to find his eyes closed and his breathing even. He's making a conscious effort to control his emotions. I reach out and run my fingers down his cheek, enjoying the smoothness of his freshly shaved skin. He shudders, and I smile softly.

"Are you ... " I have to clear my throat to keep speaking, and watch as Ty opens his eyes to look at me. "Did they charge you with anything?"

A small smile curves Ty's beautiful mouth.

"No," he says, his voice just that much lighter, that much closer to that strange ideal we all hold in such high regard: normal. For once, I'd like to just be normal. I want to bitch about dirty dishes in the sink, get annoyed with my sisters for screaming, feel nauseous from morning sickness, toss my Kindle across the room when I read a really bad cliff-hanger. And then I want to pause and think for a minute, realize how goddamn lucky I am to be bothered by any of these things, realize what a luxury it is to have so few big problems that the little things seem huge. I want to close my eyes every night and know that I'm lucky to have a place to live, a family, a baby on the way, free time enough to even read a book. Lucky enough to have Tyson Monroe McCabe.

"No," Ty repeats again, leaning forward to press his mouth to mine. "They said I was a free man, and for once in my life, I think I might actually be starting to believe that."

30

My mother's death has turned Jade's world upside down. She's so devastated that she hardly ever leaves her room, and when she does, she usually only leaves long enough to buy alcohol. When she gets back, she trudges outside, slumps down next to our mother's grave and drinks it all, until she can barely stand, until she can barely even turn herself over to vomit.

Two weeks she's been doing this, and I don't know

how to help her. Talking doesn't seem to work as everything I say falls on deaf ears. I even tried organizing some activities: baking cookies, family movie nights, walks to the park. None of it worked. If Jade participates – and that's a big *if* – then she generally just sits there in silence, staring off into the distance.

That isn't to say her reaction is wholly unique. I've caught Beth crying more times than I can count, and even though Ty and I are mostly finished emptying my mother's room, nobody will move in there. It's the biggest room in the house, and it even has an en suite bathroom. If anyone deserves it, it's Beth.

"You take it," she tells me when we have this conversation for the seventh, maybe the eighth time. Actually, she more shouts this at me. She's so paranoid about secondhand smoke that she literally counts out twenty steps between us if I'm outside when she wants a cigarette. It's stupid as hell, but I appreciate the concern.

We both glance over at Ty who's taking advantage of this one, single pseudo-sunny day in a string of grayness to bathe the dog. He's cleverly hooked up a hose to the water heater in the laundry room and run it out here, so he can bathe bitch-Angelica in luxury.

And he's doing it shirtless.

I count the number of days it's been since … *that* day and prod at the wounds on my belly. I won't be running any triathlons anytime soon, but a quickie with my husband? I think I can manage that. I bite my lip and stare at the water droplets on his smooth chest, the way they run down the grooves in his abs and soak into the waistband of his pants. *Holy fuck.* I clench my thighs together and swallow hard, trying to clear my mind of the exceptionally dirty thoughts that are running through it before Beth moves over to stand next to me, cigarette safely distinguished.

"He really is beautiful," she admits, and I can hear the longing in her voice. Not for Ty, not for my soul mate, because I know that Beth would never hurt me like that, even if I had a partner who was willing. No, she's just lonely, in love with the idea of love and trying so hard for it that she's failing miserably. Like our mother. Like I once did. Like Zella is doing now. "And he's brave, and strong, and he loves you so much." Beth pauses and looks down at her white ballet flats. Today she goes back to work at the Closing Case. I know it's already paining her to leave Darla, but Beth has a lot of pride and I know that taking money from Noah Scott is the last thing she wants to do. Unfortunately, she *has* been doing it because the legal issues my mother left in her wake are a fucking nightmare.

My mother's will does not specify a guardian for her underage children.

That means Beth has to go to court and argue for custody over my sisters. India, Lettie, Lorri, and Darla are all floating in this cosmic unknown right now. It's not a good feeling. Beth already has two young children and no partner, and we live in a conservative state. Frankly, I'm terrified for her, for them, for us.

"You take the room," she says again, and I raise an eyebrow at her. But only for a moment, of course, because Ty laughs and the sound draws my attention like nothing else. He's so fucking beautiful with his rainbow of tattoos, that sultry smile, that confidence in his eyes that I know will never shatter. "You and Ty, you're the strongest part of this family right now."

Beth's voice hitches a little when she says this.

"God, I should've married Danny when I had the chance."

My eyes snap over to hers, and I give her a look like *what the fuck are you talking about?*

"If I'd married him, we'd have money, stability." She sighs. I know she's thinking about the custody hearing again. "Maybe you should petition to be their guardians? You and Ty?"

"Me?" I ask, pointing at myself. "I'm twenty-two."

"Just take the room," Beth says, because I know right now she's wishing that *twenty* wasn't in either of our age descriptions. If she were thirty, married, successful, getting custody would be no big deal.

"Hey, there's a phone call from your work," Zella says, popping her head out the screen door. Beth looks at her for a moment and then nods before moving inside and leaving me alone with the only blonde woman in our family.

Zella steps outside and leans against the wall.

"Shouldn't you two be putting aside your differences right about now?" Zella shrugs. "With Darla and Mom and everything, this doesn't seem like it should be so important."

"I'm not going back to school," Zella blurts and my blood goes cold.

"Why the hell not?" I ask, standing up suddenly. My head spins a little and I have to force myself to take a deep breath. Zella doesn't look at me, her eyes getting caught on Ty before she turns away.

"Tobias was right. His dad cleaned up the whole

mess, wiped it away like it was never there." She laughs, but the sound is off, like a bell ringing underwater or something. "And he wants me back. Again. Even after everything I said to him, all the things we've done to each other."

"And you told him to fuck off, right?" I ask, hoping Zella isn't destined to travel the same path as the rest of us Regalis.

"I just can't go back to Texas right now. I don't want to be anywhere near him. I know he's bad for me, but I … I don't know." Zella kicks at the dirty cement of the back patio with her foot. "And I can't leave the family, not when everything is so up in the air like this. With Mom dead … and … I'm glad Darla's back, but I can't go."

"You should marry Noah and run off to Australia or some shit," Ty says, wiping water off his chest with the dog's towel, suddenly standing within hearing distance of us. I didn't even see him move, the sneaky fuck. Angelica is shaking her wet fur out and panting happily, gray and white coat gleaming in the weak sunshine. "Go, like, hang with koalas and whatever, eat some Tim Tams."

"What the fuck is a Tim Tam?" Zella asks, but Ty just shrugs, tossing the towel over his shoulder.

"You and Noah kiss and make up?" Ty asks point blank, voicing the question I've been *dying* to ask ever since I got out of the hospital.

Zella's turn to shrug.

I narrow my eyes on her.

"That means what?" I ask and she shrugs again. She's been staying at his house almost exclusively since we got

Darla back, so I had kind of assumed things were going okay. Based on her expression, I realize that might not entirely be the case.

"We haven't fucked again if that's what you're asking," she snaps, rubbing at tired, puffy eyes with the backs of her hands.

"It wasn't," I say and Ty raises an eyebrow at me.

"Speak for yourself," he mutters and I poke him in the chest teasingly. That small skin to skin touch ignites a fire inside of me and I find my mouth suddenly dry. He makes eye contact with me and inhales sharply. Need hits me like a freight train out of nowhere, and I'm left standing dumfounded on the tracks. Suddenly, I'm not so concerned with Zella and Noah and all of their problems. If they don't want this, this thing that Ty and I have, then screw 'em.

"We're taking things slowly," Zella says. I'd roll my eyes at her if they weren't already locked on Ty Ross-McCabe's. I can see the same recognition brewing in his gaze that must be rampant in mine, something that tells me I just might be able to crack him open this time. These past few weeks, he's been so careful, almost too careful. It's killing us both. We were designed to fuck, me and Ty. But hell, maybe he planned the whole 'bathing the dog' thing, just so he could be shirtless and wet and warm. Maybe he knows how good I feel today, how ready. It's the first day I've actually thought beyond *this could happen* and have settled on *this better damn well happen.* Don't know why. Don't care much either. Maybe the stars have just aligned themselves in our favor? Or maybe I'm just so sex starved at this point that I don't give a crap anymore?

I swallow hard and Ty watches my throat move like a man mesmerized.

"Go back to fucking school," he tells Zella, reaching down to grab my hand and drag me inside. As soon as the screen door slams shut, he presses me into the wall with his warm, damp body.

"How long has it been?" he whispers as I squirm, letting him pin my arms on either side of my body. "Forever and a day?"

"Feels like it," I whisper back, leaning forward for a kiss, certain that today is the day we get to break our dry spell. I'm half mad for it, for him. I want to be close, to meld our bodies together, to wash away everything that's happened with a sea of kisses, a flutter of fingers, the exquisite torture of his body moving inside of mine.

Ty barely brushes my mouth before pulling back with a cocky grin on his face. It's that look that's gotten us into this situation in the first place.

"Were you checking my ass out while I bathed the dog?"

I nod, then decide to add, "I was checking your everything out."

Ty chuckles, warm and deep, vibrating my body with the sound as he leans in close and captures my mouth. He tastes like sunshine and darkness both, like a dichotomy of flavors so raw they defy definition. I can't help myself, moaning against his lips even though I know Zella's just a few feet away. If she's learned her lesson like the rest of my family, she won't bother to come in here when she knows Ty and I are alone together.

I struggle to pull my arms from his grip, but he won't

let me, kissing me deep and slow, like a molasses drenched summer in the middle of winter. This kiss right here, right now, it's different from his others, from his hot as fuck, curl the spine, soak the panties bad boy kisses. He can still do those, of course, when he wants to, but now he can also do this, melt my heart like butter, make my knees go weak. He can kiss me like he loves me inside and out, like he's confident that'll never change. Ty kisses me like he knows he's finally come home.

I groan again and collapse back against the wall, letting him take charge, run his tongue along my teeth before drawing back just enough to nibble at my bottom lip.

"Fuck me, Ty," I groan before he can cut me off with another scalding press of his mouth. He pauses then, loosing his fingers on my wrists. I don't waste even a second in going for the button on his jeans, but Ty stops me by leaning forward and whispering in my ear.

"Come with me first, on a little outing?" he asks and I give him a look that says *you have got to be shitting me right now.* "It won't take long, and I'll make it worth your while, I swear it." Ty nips my earlobe and sends a shiver down my spine. I nod then because I'm too frustrated to speak. *Fuck a duck.* I might be pregnant, but that doesn't mean I'm not still a red-blooded woman with needs. I should pull the whole husbandly duties clause and see if that works.

Ty reaches down and wraps his left hand around mine. The bandage is gone, his burns mostly healed, but I can still see the faintest edge of raised pink, a scar that will always remind me of my mother and that horrible, awful side of her. For the other half, the part of her that was good, I have the napkin buried in my dresser drawer upstairs. Was my mother a villain like I thought? No, maybe not. No, no, I'm sure she wasn't. Life isn't that cut and dry. My mother wasn't a good guy or a bad guy, just a woman with faults. All I can really do is try to make sure that at the end of the day, I don't make the same mistakes she did.

Ty drags me upstairs and into our room, shutting the door behind us.

"Give me a sec to change, 'kay?" he says, and shoves his wet pants down his hips before I can even take a breath and ask him to stop. No, seriously, we've stopped undressing in front of one another because um, yeah, remember how we were both sex addicts? We haven't fucked in four weeks. Four weeks. I haven't gone this long without sex since … I reach my hand up to touch the chip earring.

Holy crap.

Ty pauses, buck freaking naked, damp with warm water, and looks back at me. He sees me holding the chip earring and whatever reasons he had in his head for waiting seem to go right out the window. See, when we joined SOG, we were supposed to wait six months to have sex. We didn't. When I had baby Noah, we were supposed to wait, and we didn't. Now, we're not quite at that six week mark, but … fuck it. It's my body; I get to decide when and how and where.

I decide now.

"Six weeks," Ty whispers, but I shake my head and lift my dress, showing him the healed pinkish scars on my belly – and the blue and white polka dot panties underneath. His hands clench into fists by his sides. "I

… I have news … "

"Good or bad?" I ask.

"Good," he says, voice a husky drawl, like he's absorbed some of the deep south dialect that slithers around here like a snake through grass.

"It can wait," I tell him with a sharp intake of breath. "I'm wearing a dress."

Ty moves over to me suddenly, like some sort of muscled predator, body moving like a well-oiled machine. I can't find my breath then, standing there stone still until he gets to me. He lifts his suddenly shaking hands and hovers them over my shoulders, the not quite touch of his fingers against my skin makes me bite my lip in desperation.

"I'm trying to be respectful," he chokes, even though I can see his eyes burning with heat. That, and he's fully erect and ready for me. Dear God, his heart might be telling him to wait, but his body wants to throw me over the dresser and screw me right here, doctor's instructions be damned. "I don't want to hurt you," he says, gritting his teeth and sliding his hands down my arms. I suck in a massive breath as he curls our fingers together.

"Ty, I'm fine. I feel fine. My last checkup went great." I drop his hands, curl my arms around his neck, and he growls, seriously grows a little. I shiver at the sound as I lean into him. "Don't tell me you don't want this. You forget how many times I've caught you taking care of yourself in the shower."

"Oh, that's where you're wrong," he says, putting his hands on either side of my waist; he doesn't bother to deny the accusations because they're *true*. "I *do* want this. I'm just trying to be respectful. Truthfully, I want to slam you into this wall and fuck you so hard you scream."

I lose whatever words I'd been about to say. Who needs words when there's ... this.

In response, I pull back and reach down, wrapping my fingers around the hard, needy length of him. This is the first time he's let me touch him since the surgery. Holy shit, but it feels good, almost new, like I'm a virgin all over again. I tell Ty that and he groans, taking my wrist in tight fingers and drawing my knuckles up to his lips for a kiss.

"Don't say things like that or I'm not gonna be able to control myself. Fuck, babe, we shouldn't be doing this." I kiss the side of his neck and he releases my hand, giving me a chance to reach down again, slide my fingers along his shaft.

"That's kind of the point," I whisper. Ty's eyelids flicker like a butterfly's wings as he struggles to keep his eyes from rolling back into his head. Who knew I was so good at hand jobs?

"Well, shit, if you're going to keep insisting."

I grin as Ty draws me forward by the wrist and scoops me up in his arms. I love when he does this, so I don't complain, letting my body go limp as I try to release some of the unbearable tension in my muscles.

"But we're going to take it slow, even if it kills me." Ty lays me down on the bed, hooking his fingers under the waistband of my panties as he pulls back and takes them with him. He drags the fabric down and over my dusty toes, coated with the brown midwestern earth that makes up my home. *Home.* I have a home again. *Ty* is my home. That whole *home is where the heart is* bit, it's true, so very, very true. "I'm going to be gentle, so gentle it tears my body into bits with the effort of holding back."

Ty makes a noise low in his throat and gets all my lady parts in a tizzy.

Fuck, I forgot how good this feels. I wonder if Ty's conservative attitude these past few weeks was all a front, just to get me worked up into a frenzy like this. He wouldn't let me give him a hand job, a blow job, nothing.

The anticipation has built to a crescendo, and I can hardly catch my breath.

Ty pushes my knees back, opening me up for him, kneeling off the edge of the bed and breathing his hot breath against my most sensitive spot.

"Shit." I struggle a little, try to scoot back, but Ty grips my hips with his strong fingers and tugs me closer. "I can't take it," I moan, already halfway off the edge of orgasm without even a *touch* from my beloved. Did I mention that I haven't been masturbating either? There hasn't really been time, not with all the shit we've been going through. I don't think my poor clit even remembers what it's like to be caressed, teased, tasted.

"You want this, baby," he tells me and then pauses. "I *need* this."

Ty breathes out, using his breath as a weapon, drawing it across my aching flesh, moving from thigh to thigh, up towards my belly, and then hovering back over my clit. When he lowers his lips to my cunt, I almost scream, even though he's not using tongue, kissing me as gently and as chastely as I now kiss Noah Scott on the cheek.

Jesus.

Ty kisses up and down my sensitive skin, pressing his lips to any bit of flesh he can get ahold of. When he surprises me with a small nip to my inner thigh, I jump and try to pull away. I want his cock inside of me *now.*

I tell him this and even though I can't see him, my gaze directed up at the ceiling as I struggle to hold back screams of pleasure, I know he's smirking at me.

"In due time, my dear. All in due time."

Then he's kissing me again, focusing all of his attention on my poor, neglected pussy, tasting me with a flicker of tongue. I bite my lip and squeeze my eyes shut, letting the pleasure wash over me in waves. He's good at this, too good almost.

Ty moves his tongue back to my clit, teasing with the barest flush of pleasure, convincing my body to drop all its guards, let go and give into him. It's not that hard, honestly. I gave into Ty a long, long time ago. I'm his; he's mine. That's about all there is to it.

"This is agony," I whisper, barely even able to get those words to brush past my lips. "Torture. I wish you would've slammed me into that wall." Ty laughs and the sound flutters against me like a butterfly's wings, tightening the muscles in my belly. I reach down and curl my fingers in Ty's dark hair, taking a handful of it and pulling hard as he increases the pressure of his mouth. My control withered away to nothing, I buck my hips against his face as he tightens his grip on me, ringed fingers bruising my flesh in the best possible way.

When he finally lets go, slides a hand over my belly and down, I cry out and don't care if anyone can hear me. Most of my sisters are in school right now, and the babies are all asleep in Beth's room, taking a nap. Zella has the baby monitor, so I don't let myself even worry about it. Worry is the best medicine against an orgasm, and I refuse to take a single sip.

Ty slides the fingers of his left hand into me and grunts like it's his cock instead.

"You are so tight right now, so fucking tight. Holy shit. I would've lasted, like, three seconds with this. You really are like a virgin again, aren't you?"

"Shut the fuck up," I mumble, tugging harder on his hair, bringing his face back down for another round of tongue. It's a near godlike combination, something I've experienced very few times in my life, all of them with Ty. Quickie ruts against dumpsters or in bathrooms were more my thing before. What kind of guy wants to just go down on some random chick and get nothing in return? Not the dark, tortured kind I usually went for.

Except for Ty.

Or maybe he didn't do this much before either – I never asked, and I don't want to know. It's nice to think that he does this just for me, only for me. At least I know now that whatever happened before, it doesn't matter. All that matters now is us.

"Fuck," he groans, sliding his fingers out and making me groan in disappointment. "You're clamping down so hard, I can barely move, babe."

"Screw you," I murmur as Ty climbs up between my legs and leans over, our bodies just barely touching.

"That's the idea."

Ty locks eyes with me, and my entire body goes white hot with the anticipation. Sex never meant much of anything to me before; it means a whole hell of a lot now. I can see that same realization mirrored back at me as Ty brushes my hair away from my face with ringed fingers.

"I love you, Never."

"I love you, too," I whisper, voice hardly audible above the thumping beat of my own heart.

Ty kisses me again, short and sweet, before guiding himself into me with a slow, careful motion, like he's afraid I'll break. I see the tender desperation in his eyes, the reflection of fear from that day I bled out across the driveway. He almost lost me, almost said goodbye to the one thing in this world worth living for. I feel tears prick my eyes and wrap my arms around his neck.

Ty gets the wrong idea.

The comforting pressure of his body filling mine recedes as he pulls back just a bit, just enough to make me so crazy I can't fucking stand it.

"Shit, am I hurting you, baby?" He looks down the length of my body, past the hastily shoved up fabric of my dress and right at my stomach, at the place that's both one baby's temple and the other's tomb. I suck in a harsh breath and he tries to leave. Only my arms around his neck stop him from going.

"No, no, you're not. It's not that. I ... I don't want you to hurt, make you sad. Ever. For me. Or about me." My words mimic Ty's from so long ago and he smiles.

Promise me you'll never be sad for me or about me.

A ringed hand brushes my hair back as Ty settles his weight slowly, oh so slowly, against me.

"We could move to a different position?" he suggests, but I shake my head. I wrap my legs around him and he grunts.

"I want you here, on me, over me, in me."

I lean up for a kiss and find Ty's mouth hot and

hungry and desperate for it. As soon as we make contact with our tongues, he's moving again, filling me up so deep that more tears steal out from the edges of my eyes. I've never felt as good or as free as I do in that moment. I'm starting to learn that just because bad things happen, that doesn't mean the good things are null and void. There might be a death, but there's also going to be a life to balance that out. Light for the dark, love for heartache, pleasure for pain.

Ty thrusts into me, melding our hips together, blending our spirits at the same time. His mouth doesn't leave mine as he tastes me, finds that perfect rhythm, and keeps me enthralled in the beauty of his love until we both crest that edge together, voices crying out in a symphony of dark desire.

31

Ty and I appear in the living room a few moments later looking equally disheveled, hair a mess, faces probably locked into some sort of loopy grins.

Zella raises an eyebrow – also dyed blonde – and pats little Noah's back. Big Noah is sitting on the opposite couch, one knee tucked up against his body, looking for all the world like he's just been punched in the gut. Guilt. That's the look he has right now.

Without even asking, I know why. He kicked my mother out of the cabin. He blames himself for her death, maybe even for Darla's abduction. Don't ask me how I know, I just do. Noah is too good, too kindhearted, to let something like that go as a coincidence of fate.

"You okay?" I ask him and it takes a moment for his blue eyes to lift up, slide over to mine. He looks between Ty and me and wrinkles his brow a bit. I don't miss the longing gaze he slides over to Zella.

"Fine."

His voice is off, so unlike Noah, like he's absorbed some darkness of his own.

"Could you watch the babies for a bit?" I ask, feeling guilty for even bringing it up. Zella shouldn't be here watching my kids, Beth's kids, mom's kids. She should be at school. Hell, she should be in the barn rutting with Noah fucking Scott. But Ty has 'news' that he wants to tell me, and damn it, but I want to hear about it. He says he won't tell me though until he can *show* me. "Just for now. We'll be back pretty quick."

Chuck Norris the cat appears on the edge of the couch and sits down, wrapping his tail around his body and licking his shoulder like he thinks I'm full of shit. Whatever. I give him a pat anyway.

"No problem," Zella says as I move over and take my baby for a moment, hold him against my chest and breathe him in. He smells good, like milk and sugar or something. It's a stupid thought, but I cling to it anyway. Mini McCabe and me, we're still a work in progress, but we're getting better. I'm not about to go shopping at the babyGap (shudder), but I can hold him now, smile at him, feed him without those strange feelings of fear and disappointment and guilt.

That's a damn good start for me.

I turn to Ty and he wraps his arms around me, around us, me and his baby. He holds us there for a full, perfect minute before planting a kiss on his son's head and handing him back to Zella for me. Today, Mini McCabe is sporting a fairy costume, with tiny gossamer wings on his back and everything. Of course, he's more of a 'dark fairy' or some shit, dressed in black and red the color of blood. Ty dressed him, can you tell?

"Thanks, Zella," I say as I move away and watch her smile blandly at me. As soon as we get outside, I lean over and whisper to Ty. "We have to do something about those two idiots." He nods and reaches into his pocket for a smoke … only he doesn't have one. His mouth twitches and he scrunches up his brow as we make our way over to Zella's car. We're going to have to remedy that soon, get a car of our own somehow.

I swipe some orange and black hair behind my ear. It's about time to change the color. Now all I have to do is decide on a new one.

"An intervention may be required," Ty says, stepping up to the car and opening the door for me. I smile at his dark chivalry and plant a kiss on his cheek, pausing when he reaches down and wraps a hand around my wrist. "Something that'll induce a situation between them like the one we had upstairs." I shiver, but Ty isn't about to let go. He'll never let go, not really. And that's okay, fine, perfect even, but I'll never let go of him either. "I can still taste you on my lips."

I roll my eyes and climb into the car, pulling him down into a crouch beside me.

"You're trying too hard. You don't need pickup lines anymore. You had me at six pack abs and beautiful eyes." I stick my tongue out at him and he laughs, stretching his arms above his head, so I can get a tantalizing peek at those said ab muscles.

"You think I have beautiful eyes?" he asks, pausing the conversation as he moves over to climb into the driver's seat.

"The most," I admit, and Ty grins. "I'd like them even better if you'd smoke a post coital cig for me?" I bat my eyelashes in a way that just feels *wrong*. Ugh. I might be head over heels in love, but I still can't do the cutesy stuff all that well. I'm just too much of an ornery bitch, I guess.

Ty chuckles and pats his pockets down.

"But I ain't got none, babe," he says and then salutes me. "Scout's honor. I dumped my whole stash." Ty covers his face with both hands. "Even my *kreteks,*" Ty says with a groan, referring to those delicious smelling clove cigs we're so obsessed with. I think they have, like, glass in them or something. So bad for the lungs. So good for the soul. "It feels so weird to fuck and not smoke."

"I know."

He drops his hands and looks over at me, reaching over to curl our fingers together.

"We'll just have to nurture some sins in our quest to snuff out others." He lifts my hand to his lips and presses a smoldering kiss to my knuckles, all the while holding eye contact with me in the most intimate way possible.

I find myself licking my lips, trying to wet my

suddenly dry mouth. *Holy fuck.* No wonder I got pregnant again. When Ty looks like this, smirks like this, touches me like this, I can't think clearly. Must be some biological fuck up, right? Some secret plan by nature to make sure I breed – a lot. Ugh. Lacey has no idea how lucky she is.

"Still trying to withhold this news from me?" I ask as Ty releases my hand with agonizing slowness, scraping the whorls of his fingertips against my skin. He has a wicked look that makes my insides feel like they're being scrambled up. I get dizzy for a second and realize I've forgotten to breathe. "I thought we had an honesty policy?"

"We do," he says, starting the car with a smile quirking the corner of his lips. "And I'm going to be honest, just as soon as I show you. I have to show you, Nev, because then it means more than words."

What the hell am I supposed to say to that?

I cross my arms over my chest and watch Ty's face as he pulls out of the driveway, just because I want to, just because I like looking at him. That's how much I care. Even if we could never touch again, I would want to be by his side anyway, to hear his laugh, his voice, see his smiles. It'd be worth it.

We only go maybe a mile or two before Ty turns on his blinker and takes us down another gravel road, towards an empty house with a wraparound porch and a *for sale* sign. My heart starts to pound in my throat.

"Ty."

He chuckles softly and takes us all the way down the private gravel drive, lined in trees and hedges, like this place is completely cut off from the rest of the world. It's within walking distance from the Regali stronghold and yet I had no idea it was even here.

"You didn't." Ty has a tendency to do things behind my back – good things, necessary things – but things. You know, like making appointments for us to get tested, signing us up for SOG, re-enrolling us both in school ... buying a house?

He chuckles softly as we pause in front of the red brick steps of the porch. The yard here is nothing like the one at my mother's, like that flat, grass covered neglected nothingness. This one is filled with plants who look suspiciously as if they're sleeping, waiting for winter to end. I recognize the leaves of a limelight hydrangea, a cluster of frost-proof gardenias, and a Chinese snowball. Even in the fall, I bet this yard is absolutely stunning, like something from a fairytale.

"No, I didn't. Not yet. But guess what I did get?" Ty pulls some keys from his pocket and jingles them around. "Did you know the realtors 'round here kind of like me? I made some friends when I was passing out flyers for Darla." I lean back and raise an eyebrow at Ty.

"You mean you flirted and charmed your way into some friends, right?" He just smiles again and turns off the ignition.

"Anyway, one of the realtors gave me these keys and told me to take a look at my leisure. I wanted to show you the house before I made a move. Nev, I want to be your partner. I want to make every decision with you, no matter how big or small. I've been alone for so long that I'm not all that great at it, but it's all I really give a flying fuck about right now." Ty twirls the keys around on one of his ringed fingers, making me unconsciously reach up to rub my own. He's wearing all silver and white today, the jewels on his fingers shining like diamonds. I mean, they might be. I still don't know every detail of his story, but that's okay because we have forever together for me to learn it. And besides, I'm finally starting to figure out how much more important the present is than the past. I'm not saying we should just fuck off and forget about it or anything, just that living in the moment isn't simply a clichéd phrase – it's the ultimate truth.

"You don't want to go all alpha male and tie me up in the basement instead?" I joke because I'm suddenly choking on all of the feelings rising up inside of me. I lost my baby, then I found one, lost my mother, lost my sister, found her. But that's life, I suppose, all over the place. Never neat, always messy. I guess this is just what a Never ever after looks like.

"Hmm," Ty purrs for a moment, leaning close to me. I lean into him and we press our cheeks together. "Nah. I don't see the fucking point in all that. It's easy to ask, to try, to even make someone yours, but it's a hell of a lot more difficult to ask them to take you as theirs. And that's what I fucking want, Never. I want to be yours."

"You are mine," I promise, tilting my head for a perfect kiss. "And I am yours. So you got your wish. Now, you better fucking spill and explain this to me." I point at the house because I'm getting excited, even though I shouldn't be. We can't afford this place. Right?

"That offer we got on the house?" Ty teases and I feel my eyes widen. A part of me is afraid to hear his answer, afraid to let go of that place where we really, truly became a family, but the rest of me is excited, anxious to start a new life here, in this place where I once thought my life had ended for good. "The sellers got all their shit together. It's a go, babe, a green light. And they have a baby on the way." He leans over again and gives me a look. "You know, kind of like us." Ty splays his ringed fingers over my belly and my breath catches. "So they want to close quick, in like thirty days." He looks out my window at the house, sitting all quiet and pretty in the icy sunshine of this most perfect winter day. "And for whatever reason, it seems like houses in New York sell for a hell of a lot more than ones in Mississippi. Come on. Get out. Let's be adults and tour a *house*."

I feel my heart start to pound as Ty pulls away, and open my door as quick as I can, practically stumbling up the steps as we race for the doorknob. Ty grabs me at the last moment and swings me around, tucking me close to him and holding me so tight all the breath leaves my body.

Breathless. Broken. But not destroyed.

I pull back and notice that Ty has a small bag hanging from his arm. Whatever's in that, I have no clue.

"What the fuck are you up to now?" I ask as he bites his lip seductively and opens the door, letting it swing inward and holding out a hand.

"Enter at your own risk," he growls, and even though he's being stupid and silly as hell, I get goose bumps on the back of my neck. My body is sweetly sore down below, reminding me that I'm not safe from Ty anymore. Oh no, I'm in reckless, beautiful danger, and it feels so good. Yet another reason why I donned the same dress from earlier. I wouldn't mind getting lucky again today.

I step inside the cool darkness of the house, my feet moving across old wood floors, a little rough around the edges but bursting with charm and character. To my left is a living room cloaked in shadow from the previous owner's drapes. Without hesitating, I move over and swing them wide, feeling a small thrill inside of me.

I'm like, a grown up and shit. A chill travels down my spine. I'm only twenty-two, but I have a baby and a half, a husband ... we sold our *house.* I wrinkle my nose.

"This could be ours," Ty says, sliding his arms around my waist and leaning into me. I close my eyes and listen to the quiet echo of silence all around us. It's punctuated with the beautiful beating rhythm of our hearts. I slide my fingers along Ty's butterfly tattoos and sigh, not a sigh of discontent, but a sigh of strength. "Close enough to your sisters, far enough away." I smile. "A room for each baby, a kitchen that needs work but," Ty laughs against my ear and I shiver, "has all working appliances. Oh, and the roof doesn't leak." He nibbles my ear and then steps back, leaving me cold and aching for him.

I spin around and lean back against the bay window, looking up at the ceiling, at the dusty fan waiting to spin on a hot, lazy summer day.

"Can we really afford this?" I ask and Ty nods, setting his bag down on the floor and pulling out my laptop. He fiddles with it for a moment and then stands up to set it on the mantle above the brick fireplace. I raise an eyebrow because I'm not sure what he's up to. Whatever it is, I know it's going to be ridiculous – and probably fucking precious as hell.

Do I really deserve all of this?

I kick my little monster square in the teeth and tell her to shut the hell up. *I am worth it.*

"I told you, I have strangely beautiful credit." Ty

pauses and taps his ringed fingers against the mantle in a steady rhythm before glancing over his shoulder to look at me. "And this house really does cost, like, half of the one in New York. And it has acres, babe. *Acres.* Space. Just mine and yours. No memories, no ghosts, just a new start for all of us."

Ty presses a button and music blares out of the speakers, filling the empty room with a colorful sea of notes and rhythms.

It's *Black Velvet* by Alannah Myles.

Wow.

Ty really does listen to me.

"Be spontaneous with you?" I joke as tears fill my eyes. Ty knows I miss my mom, even if it's just a little bit, even if I'm too afraid to admit that to myself.

When he holds out his hand, I take it and let him wrap me up in his warmth, his strength, his confidence. I don't even need to see the rest of the house to know I'm in love. If Ty likes it, I like it. I like *this.*

He spins us in slow, lazy circles, in time with the music and doesn't even care that I'm getting his shirt wet with my tears. When I drop my head into the crook of his neck, he starts to hum the song under his breath, sending warm vibrations through his chest and into me.

I sob harder.

It's a cleansing cry only, not a sad one. How could I be sad with Ty McCabe holding me in his strong, beautiful arms? The same arms that hold our son and rock him to sleep, that punched my father's murderer out, that caress me in all the right places. I owe a lot to these hands, these arms, truly, I do. I owe them my life.

"Let the tears flow, Mrs. McCabe, just let 'em all out."

"It's Ross-McCabe," I correct with a sniffle and Ty laughs. We continue to spin in slow, slow circles, traveling the length of the room and back. To anyone else, our dance probably looks stupid as hell. To me, it's a grand waltz, danced in the ballroom of hard fought battles and against all odds love.

"I miss the baby I never had," I say again and Ty nods, squeezing me even tighter, until I'm not even a hundred percent certain my feet are touching the ground. "I miss my mom."

"I know."

He kisses the top of my head and we stay there until the song is over and there's nothing but the sound of silence and the blur of a distant sun leaking through the open window.

32

When we get home, Zella and Noah are still sitting the living room. They must not hear us come in at first because Ty and I can hear them arguing, even as the screen door squeaks shut behind us.

"Why, Zella?" Noah asks, and I know him well enough to recognize that pleading sense of desperation in his voice. "Why not give me a chance to prove myself to you? Prove that you're my number one?"

"You didn't stand up to my mother, not until she had the audacity to pick on Never." Zella's voice is quiet and sure, like she's thought a hell of a lot about this. *Fuck.* My sister is being an idiot. I want to march in there and deal with this myself, but Ty grabs my arm and pulls me back.

"We can eavesdrop, but we don't interfere," he whispers, and since he's apparently the god of gossip, I listen to him. Or maybe it's because he's the god of everything in my eyes. At least he's the god of sex ... he proved that to me in the empty house, after I balled my eyes. Fucker. He was just waiting to seduce me.

"You defended Never, and then you drove my mother away, and then she died," Zella says, her voice breaking down with each word she speaks. I feel my entire body stiffen. Can't she see the guilt and fear in Noah's eyes? This is the thing he fears the most, to be blamed for what happened. But it wasn't his fault, not by a long shot. And he didn't stand up for *me,* he stood up for the entire family. It wasn't me specifically that spurred his actions, just a lot of little things boiling up into a crescendo. Can't Zella see that? Or maybe she simply *won't.* She wants to suffer, to be unhappy, we all do. It's a Regali trait. "You killed my mother, Noah," Zella says, her voice thick with tears. "On accident, maybe, but you did."

If she's going to start the blame game, then she should be blaming Ty for Darla's disappearance, me for running away and fucking Jade up, hell, even Autumn and Maple for tying Beth to Danny. The blame game never turns out well for anybody.

"I'm sorry, Zella," Noah whispers, and I hear his

footsteps moving across the floor. "I didn't know that would happen. I was just ... I was so fed up with the abuse that I couldn't take it anymore. If your mom had done what she did to Never to you, I would've ... I would've done something a whole hell of a lot worse. Please, understand, I *love* you. I've loved you for a long time now. I've never lied to you before, so why would you doubt me now?"

"You should go," Zella says, putting a false strength into her voice that I know she doesn't feel.

"Is it Tobias?" Noah asks quietly.

"GET OUT!" Zella screams, and both Ty and I cringe. I can't take it anymore, so I untangle myself from my dark butterfly, and move forward, only to run straight into Noah. His face is white as a sheet, eyes haunted, a total wreck.

"Sorry, Nev," he whispers, taking my shoulders and gently moving me aside. He grabs his coat from the rack and disappears out the door before I can get in a single word.

"Your baby's sleeping upstairs in Autumn's crib," Zella murmurs, shoving the baby monitor against my chest before she, too, disappears, up the stairs this time.

"Fuck me sideways," Ty says, reaching for a cigarette. Only, once again, there's none there. "You got a bow and arrow we could use? Some love potion number nine? It's like Zella wants to make drama, like she doesn't have enough."

"It's genetic," I mumble, dropping the baby monitor by my side. I listen as Noah's tires squeal across the gravel drive and then fade away into the distance. Hmm.

"Do you think he needs some sex advice?" I raise a

brow and toss a look over my shoulder. "Kidding," Ty says, raising his hands, palm out, in surrender. "You know I heart the fuck out of that little bastard." My husband's mouth twitches. "Even though he popped my wife's cherry."

I snort.

"You're disgusting," I say, pausing as a door opens upstairs and Darla, Lettie, and Lorri appear. Ah. We were at the house so long that school's out now. Holy shit. Ty can be like a time vortex sometimes. A day with him can pass as quickly as a minute, maybe because I never want it to end.

"Will you play *Rock Band* with us?" Lettie asks, making a face that's almost too sexy for her age. Jesus. Fourteen is a terrible place to be, trapped between child and teen. I'm going to have to keep my eye on this one.

"Uh, of course," Ty says, capturing Darla as she comes down the stairs, hoisting her up and hugging her with as much love, as much care, as he does his own son. I love the fuck out of him for that.

"My turn first!" Lettie says, pushing Lorri out of the way. "I want to sing *Lucky* by Britney Spears. I listened to it on YouTube today. It's my new favorite song now." Crap. I'm going to have to keep a *really* close eye on that one.

"That song isn't even on the game, stupid," Lorri says as Ty reaches down and takes my hand. We smile at each other, and I'm sure I'm in for a beautiful, lazy, family filled afternoon.

Only, my life isn't that easy, is it?

"NEVER!" Zella's exploding from her bedroom and stumbling at the top of the stairs. She almost pitches forward and just barely manages to recover, waving a note around as she flies down the staircase at a speed that terrifies the shit out of me. Ty grabs her with his left arm, keeping Darla in the other, as Zella trips on the last step. Tears are streaming down her face and she looks like she's suddenly developed a really bad case of PTSD. "Jade is gone. She left, Never. Jade left. Oh my God, no. This can't happen again. This isn't happening again."

I snatch the note from my sister's hand, dizziness sweeping up and over me. *History repeats itself.* Would my sister really make such a stupid decision? Would she really imitate me on the worst level possible? No. No. No.

My eyes scan the note again, and again, and again.

"When's the last time you saw her?" I ask Zella as my sister sobs freely, terrifying the shit out of Lettie and Lorri. Darla, too, starts to cry, and I don't blame her. We just lost our mother, almost lost her. Fuck. Even I gave them all a scare when I collapsed on the driveway. Would Jade really inflict more pain on our family?

"I don't know. Like an hour ago?" Zella rubs at her blonde hair like she's trying to think. "Two? Noah and I were … we argued for a long time. I have no idea. I don't know. I tried her cell, but she won't answer. I texted her, too. Nothing."

"Fuck." I can feel my hands starting to shake. Somehow, I feel like this is my fault, like I should've done more to ease Jade's suffering. I drop the note, but Ty catches it in midair, pausing to set Darla down and stroke her hair back.

"It'll be okay, button, I promise." He looks up and waggles his brows at the other girls. "Go start the game without me and I'll be right there. Everything's fine."

"Last time you said that, our mother died," Lettie says, her face filling with tears. She turns and runs down the hallway, disappearing into the den. Nobody goes after her though, because we're all too occupied with the note.

I'm sorry to do this to you all, but I have to put myself first. Please don't judge me for it – you didn't judge Never. I ask for that same respect. Maybe when I come home, I can be happy and carefree, too. But I'm tired of being the outcast, and now that Mom is gone, I have no friends in that house. Please understand. It was this or suicide.

"Shit," Ty says, sucking his lower lip under his teeth. "She can't have gone far, right? Not in an hour or two." He snatches a coat off the rack and slips it over his shoulders. "I'll go look for her."

"Me, too," Zella says, swiping the tears off her face. "This is partly my fault. I didn't notice her leave. I'm coming with you."

I start to open my mouth, but Ty spins and takes my face between his hands.

"I want you to stay here, baby. Call Beth, let her know. I'll text you updates on my phone."

I struggle internally for a moment and then realize how stupid I'm being. Someone has to stay with the kids, and I'm pregnant, still weakened from the surgery. It's obvious that I'm the one who should stay.

I nod, even though it kills me.

I follow Ty and Zella outside, down the porch steps and pause on the driveway with them as an unfamiliar truck rumbles down the road. It pauses about twenty feet from where Ty is standing, and we all watch as a man climbs out the passenger side, not even bothering to shut the door behind him.

"Can I help you?" Ty asks, his body going stiff as the man walks toward us in a pair of nondescript jeans, black T-shirt. He's not much to look at it, not particularly remarkable, not that threatening at first glance. But Ty is worried. I can see it in the set of his shoulders.

I move down the steps and take a position by his side, even though I can see that's freaking him out. He steps in front of me, just a little.

"You Tyson?" he asks, and Ty pushes me back with his left hand, the hand that will be forever scarred because of his love for me.

"Who the fuck wants to know?" he says, his voice dark and dangerous.

In an instant, the situation escalates beyond even my wildest imagination. This man in front of Ty, he pulls a knife, and I feel the entire world wash away in black and white, all color drained.

"TY!" I scream, trying to go for him, to help him.

The knife hits Ty straight in the stomach, even though he moves fast, faster than I even thought possible. With a grunt, the man jerks the knife back and simultaneously gets hit in the face with a fistful of rings. He drops like a fucking sack, crumpling to the driveway with a groan, and seconds later, the truck starts to pull out of the driveway, door still hanging wide.

"Call an ambulance!" I shout at Ty, wondering why everything, fucking *everything* has to come full circle. I'm okay with the sex, and the babies, and the jokes, and all of the family drama, but why, when I was just left lying on a driveway bleeding out, does it have to happen to the man I love, too? What the fuck world? Why? Why? Why? "Ty," I reach out to grab him, but he's not done. He leans down, blood pouring dark and heavy from his wound, and snatches the man by his shirt. Ty hits him again, keeping him upright, even as I try to tug on his arm, to pull him away, examine his wound.

"Ty, listen to me," I whisper, but his eyes are dark now, twisted up in shadows. He hits the guy again, so hard that I hear a crack and then lets him go, stumbling back and landing on his ass in front of me.

I crawl up to him, try to press my hands to the oozing brightness of his wound. With a detached look blooming on his face, Ty reaches down and touches his ringed fingers to the red, lifting them up for inspection.

"Fuck," he whispers, the darkness fading from his eyes, taking them back to that perfect brown, that maple syrup, that sweet chocolate. My breath chokes in my throat. "Hannah," he says, as if in explanation, and I know immediately what he's talking about. This is retribution for talking to the cops. But no. No. No. This stuff doesn't happen in real life, can't happen in real life.

Now, for the first time ever, I really truly understand what Ty went through when I was in the hospital, and it is fucking *terrifying*. And I selfishly thought dying was bad. This is worse. So much worse.

"Don't leave me, baby," I whisper as Zella stumbles out the front door, shouting that the ambulance is on its way. Fast. Faster. Fastest. *Please hurry.* "It's going to be alright. It is. It will." I press a kiss to Ty's forehead, his cheek, his mouth, before ripping off my hoodie and using it to press against his wound.

"I won't leave you, Nev, I swear it." He raises his bloody hand up and draws his fingers down my cheek. "I promise."

What I don't say, but that I'm thinking, is that you should Never make promises you're not sure you can keep.

To Be Continued...

Never Could Stop (Tasting Never #7) ~ Coming soon!

Sign up for

C.M. Stunich's newsletter
and get all the latest updates on new releases!

Sign up at: http://goo.gl/vfw2m2
your email will not be sold or shared with anyone

*If you enjoyed this, you might like
"Stepbrother Inked"
by debut author Violet Blaze*

*Keep going to read the sample
chapters!*

VIOLET BLAZE

STEPBROTHER

PROLOGUE

Three years earlier...

I curled my own fingers around my throat and bit back a gasp. *It shouldn't feel so good to be touched like this.* The hand wrapped around my own was firm, but insistent. There was no way I was getting out of it this time.

"Flor." The word dropped from my lips like a cinder, one that I thought had gone cold but that always managed to flair back to life in a surge of heat and desire that I knew was wrong. Knew it. But couldn't stop the fire from fanning itself into a raging flame.

My brother – sorry, my *stepbrother* because let's be

honest here, there's a big difference – pulled me forward so forcefully that I stumbled, fingers still at my throat in a gesture of surprise. *What,* exactly, he was doing here, I wasn't sure, but the hard glint in his eyes and the firm set of his mouth told me what I feared most: that he still, and maybe always would, think of me as a sister. If he didn't, then why was he so angry? Why did his full lips twist down in a scowl at the corners? And why was his grip so hard and his aura so … messy. His emotions twisted down his arm, following the colorful lines of his tattoos as they wrapped his bicep, bleeding into me and choking back my breath. Messy. I couldn't tell if he was just pissed or if he was disappointed, too, if maybe he couldn't believe he'd just caught me with a boy's arms around my waist and his tongue in my mouth. I was supposed to be the good one, right? The one that didn't give my dad or my stepmom any trouble because Flor gave them more than they could handle.

His dark hair bled into his eyes, dripping with sweat from the heat of the party and the crush of bodies, and I stared in simple fascination as he swept it back and glared at me.

"What the *fuck*," he began as I cringed, "are you doing here?" I watched in horror as my stepbrother's gaze lifted and met that of the boy's behind me. I kept one hand on my neck, sliding it down to my chest so that I could feel the rapid thump and slam of my heart, much like the chilling bass beat that was tingling up my toes and making me blissfully deaf. Maybe then I wouldn't have to hear the sound of my father's disappointment when he sighed and then later probably screamed at me for this little adventure? "And *who*," Florian continued, "the fuck is that?"

"None of your business, bro," my mystery date said, curling his own fingers around my hip in a strange mockery of the way I'd done to my own throat, caught up in surprise when Flor had appeared out of nowhere and pulled me from my make out session and back to the harsh, gritty twang of reality. "Hey, are you alright?" the guy asked me as I glanced over my shoulder and swallowed hard. I guess he mistook my speechlessness for fear because he stepped around me and got in Flor's face. "You can't make her leave if she doesn't want to go."

"I can," Flor snapped back at him, grinding his teeth and squeezing my wrist even tighter than before, "if she's my sister." He leaned in and let my date have it with a simple whisper of words. "Oh, by the way, she's only fifteen, asshole." My new friend tore his hand away from my hip like it was on fire – but not the good kind, not the kind I was feeling right now as Flor's sweaty fingers tugged me forward. No, this was more like he was *terrified* of me now, like he wouldn't touch me with a ten-foot pole. I guessed he wouldn't want to, considering he was twenty-one. Guess I shouldn't have lied about my age.

"Hey, Flor," a girl with long black hair and brightly colored extensions giggled as we passed by. "You in a hurry or something?" She eyed me with no small amount of contempt as Flor dragged me through the crowd and paused only when we were standing on the porch outside the little green and white house. In the middle of a neighborhood known locally as The Whit, it was unlikely the cops would get called on this place, so it was a hotspot for parties. I knew because I'd followed Flor here more than once. Tonight, though, tonight I'd really believed him when he'd told his mom he – and I quote – *felt like shit* and was going upstairs to lie down. Florian never lied about going to parties. He just ... went. No matter what sort of fight his mom put up.

"Yeah, I sort of am," he growled, ignoring the girl and pulling me down the steps in my heels. His broad back filled my view, blocking the clusters of teenagers and young adults hanging out on the sidewalk at the bottom of the steps. The fabric stretched across his muscles in a way that was criminal. I was young, sure, but I wasn't so young that I couldn't appreciate that, couldn't appreciate the way Flor's body had changed from a lanky teenage boy's to a ... to a *man's*.

I flushed from head to toe and rolled my eyes. I'd binged last week during spring break, reading each and every single one of the romance novels crammed onto my stepmom's shelf. It was part curiosity, I guess, that encouraged me to read them. That, and part disappointment and frustration that Flor got to go away and I didn't. Since then I'd been saying and thinking strange things, like how Flor always smelled so good. Or how I was glad he didn't shut his bedroom door when he was changing his shirt. That kind of stuff.

I looked away from Florian's back to stare at the pavement for a moment, trying to pull myself together. If he was a mess of emotions then so was I. Nervous, anxious, frustrated ... jealous. I swallowed hard and glanced back over at the girl. She was standing with her arms crossed over her flat chest, her lips pursed, looking from Flor's face to his hand, the one that was wrapped around my wrist, and then back again.

"You brought me here," she said accusingly, the fabric of her black dress reflecting the light from the flickering street lamp above us. I watched her eyes as they moved over my stepbrother, taking in each and every line of his body like she was lost in the desert and he, he was a nice, tall glass of water. When her eyes moved over to me, I saw a primal response, a surge of jealous anger that made me swallow twice – not because I was scared but because I was *angry*. Didn't she know that Flor didn't belong to anyone? He said that all the time when his mother asked why he never brought girls home. Then, of course, he'd whisper under his breath that he actually brought girls home *all* the time, only that she didn't notice.

I tried to pull my arm from Florian's grasp, but he wouldn't let go of me.

"This isn't a good time," he said, pausing to glance over at me. I refused to meet his eyes. I didn't know how to feel towards him. Why was it okay for *him* to party, to kiss whoever he wanted, to … do whatever with whoever he wanted? I had a right to experiment, too. "This is my sister." I cringed again, hating the way he said that word. *Sister.* I wasn't his sister and hadn't even known him as long as I'd known my best friend, Addison. Florian and I had met ten years ago and had only lived together full time for eight of them. "I've got to get her home, okay?" I looked back at the girl and saw her face soften. Sister. The word always did that to them, like I was no longer a threat. Because, of course, Florian would never want anything to do with me. I wasn't a girl to him, just an obligation. I was *safe.* "And then maybe I'll be back after," he added which did nothing to enhance the slowly building smile on the girl's face. Her red lips turned down and she rolled her eyes, spinning on her heels and marching up the white steps we'd just come down.

"Abigail," Flor said, and I swallowed again, this time to get past the lump in my throat. I wished he'd let go of me; that would've made things easier. "Let's go." But Florian didn't release me and instead, pulled me towards his car, double parked next to a white Honda Civic, its silver paint dull in the shadowy corridor of the street. Only two street lamps on either side of the house worked; the rest had been broken sometime in the last few years. "Get in," he said, finally letting go of my arm. I spun then, surprising him, tears welling up unbidden from God only knows where.

"Why?" I asked him and it was his turn to roll his eyes and shake his head, like he knew better, like *he* had room to talk. He reached out to take my arm again, but I stepped back, pulling it out of his reach. He mistook my emotions for fear and opened the car door with a sigh.

"I won't tell your dad," he said as he tilted his head to the side and watched me. The eyebrow ring in his left brow winked as a car behind us turned on its headlights and pulled forward, zooming around Florian's illegally parked Mazda like it didn't even exist, like we were in our own little world. "If that's what you're freaking out about, don't worry."

I watched him watching me, drank in the details of that moment, the way his eyes were focused wholly and completely on mine, the way his tongue brushed against his lower lip, the way his newest tattoo – a girl with a wolf skin draped over her shining brown curls – gleamed with lotion and a dabbling of sweat.

"Why do you get to have all the fun?" I asked, and I knew I sounded exactly the way I didn't want to sound – like

I really was fifteen. "Why do you get to bring girls over to the house when Dad and River are at work? Why do you get to go to parties on school nights and disappear over spring break, long enough that your mom actually thinks about calling the cops?" I wrapped my arms around myself and took another step back as Florian's eyes narrowed.

"You're fifteen, Abi," he said, confirming my worst fear. Eighteen year old Florian knew everything and here I was, his whiny younger sister who played the cello and had just had her first kiss with some stranger. He probably thought I was crazy. "Get in the car and let's go home."

"No," I said and he growled low under his breath, sending a chill straight up my spine. A cool breeze drifted down between the houses on either side of us, teasing my skirt and bringing goose bumps up on my exposed thighs. Florian's school blazer was hanging loosely from my shoulders, but not because he'd given it to me. Because I had decided to go to the party in my school uniform the way the rest of the girls did and wanted to wear burgundy – the color of the senior class.

"Why are you being so goddamn stubborn?" he snarled at me, running a hand through his sweaty hair. I wondered briefly how long he'd been at the party before he'd found me. "Do you *want* me to call your dad and tell him you're here?"

"Do whatever you want," I snapped back, taking a step towards him this time. I needed him to know I wasn't going to back down without an answer. I watched as he scowled and shoved his hands in his front pockets, looking down at me as he sucked in a deep breath. I could tell he was pissed but trying not to show it. His eyes, green and sharp as thorns, took me in from head to toe, pausing at the black and white skull patterned socks I'd pulled up to my knees. Those definitely weren't regulation for Mercy High School students, but I'd worn them anyway and scraped by without detention for it. I'd even rolled the waistband of my skirt up a few times, hiding the bunched fabric by pulling my white dress shirt out and letting it hang loose – another fashion statement I'd never participated in before today. I could tell Florian noticed. "I'm not going home, Flor. I want to stay." He looked up at my face then and took his own step forward, the toes of our shoes just this side of touching.

I tried not to meet his eyes, keeping my gaze on the bleeding rose pattern that decorated his shirt, convinced that I could see every muscle in his chest and belly through the tight fabric.

"You're my sister," he said, and this time, when I cringed, he noticed. "I'm not leaving you at some second-rate, shitty party to get taken advantage of."

"It's not your decision," I whispered as his hands came up and touched my elbows, sliding to my shoulders and pulling the blazer down my arms. Flor's face was ridiculously close to mine when he leaned in and tossed the jacket onto the front seat. I could feel the warm brush of his breath against my lips, like an indirect kiss, a ghost of a wish that would never come true. "And I'm not your sister."

Then I did look up at him, meeting his green eyes with my blue ones and trying not to let him see how nervous I felt, how his nearness and his touch undid me. The things I felt for him, that I didn't feel for any other guy, they were wrong. I knew that. I *knew* that. Still, it didn't matter. He *wasn't* my brother and I was about three-fifths sure I was in love with him.

"I know."

I thought for one brief second there that Flor was really going to kiss me. I could practically taste his mouth, smell the scent of his shampoo, could practically *feel* that cinder on my tongue burning against his, igniting some sort of ... blaze between us that would burn us both to ashes.

But he didn't.

He didn't kiss me, just took a step back and went around to the driver's side of the car, opening his door and leaning on the roof with his arms crossed. His face was smooth-shaven, but the shadows from the trees looming above us played tricks on my mind and made it look like he had stubble across his jaw, rough and untamed. My eyes managed to find the single scar on his chin, the one he'd gotten from a bike ride gone wrong, even in the dim lighting. I focused on that instead of his eyes.

"Up to you," he said, and his voice was easy to hear, even with the pulsing thump of music radiating from the old Craftsman. Flor always had a sharp, clear voice and a tone that brooked no argument, not even from his own mother. It was like he just knew *everything,* and that annoyed me. "Come with me now or I'll follow you back inside and tell everyone that you're fifteen. Then they can kick you out themselves and you can wait on the street corner for your dad to pick you up."

"I hate you," I whispered, even though that wasn't true.

Flor nodded like the know-it-all jerk he was and climbed into the car.

I followed after him, slamming my door to let him know I didn't like this and that I was *pissed.*

"I really hate you," I said again, brushing away a slight

swell of tears with an angry hand.

"Yeah, I'm a real piece of shit," he told me as I slammed my foot on the dashboard and left it there, resting my cheek against my thigh as I gazed out the window. There was a long pause before Flor started the car and when I glanced over, I caught him staring at me. I narrowed my eyes and looked away again before he could see how hurt I was, how desperate I was for his attention.

Then the engine started and we were whizzing through the city and towards South Hills, towards the four bedroom house that I spent most of my free time in, reading and doing massive amounts of AP homework. Neither of us spoke as Flor drove me home.

When we got there, I shoved open my door before Flor had even put the car in park and stormed up to the front porch, tugging down the hem of my skirt as I went. Even if Flor didn't rat me out – which I wasn't at all sure about – my outfit might give me away.

I raced up the cement steps to the dark green door and pushed it open, hearing my stepmom's laughter ring down the staircase. She and Dad were probably upstairs *snuggling* and watching their evening movie. They always made time for it, no matter what happened. I sort of envied them their relationship. Must be nice to have someone to hang out with all the time. All I had was a best friend who'd just moved nine hundred miles away and a stepbrother that hated me.

"Hey," Flor said, reaching out and grabbing at my arm again. The front door shut softly behind him as I turned, looking down at his fingers curled around my bicep. He licked his lips again and for a split second there, he looked almost nervous. "I meant what I said, you know. I won't tell your dad a thing." I didn't respond. "But that doesn't mean I like what I saw."

"Like I enjoy finding you with your hands up girls' shirts on the living room couch." I started to pull away again, but Flor pulled me back. I spun around, intending to give him a piece of my mind and found him way too close to me, smelling too good, breathing too hard, eyes even sharper than normal.

"You never said anything before," was all he said, and since I didn't know how to respond to that, I decided to be flippant.

"Why should I? It should be obvious. What sister likes to see her brother going at it with a different girl every weekend?"

Flor stared at me for a good long moment, fingers still curled around my arm and then suddenly, he was pushing me against the wall, pinning my arms above my head with his right hand, and molding our bodies together in a way that brought a small moan tumbling unbidden from my lips.

"I thought you said you weren't my sister," he whispered, and then he really did press his lips to mine, slide his tongue into my mouth. I wanted to slap him or scream for joy or run upstairs and call Addison or knee him in the balls or … I found myself arching my breasts against his chest, my mouth moving against his. I melted into Flor as he leaned into me, one knee between my legs, barely keeping me from sliding to the floor in a puddle of surprise and … pleasure. *It really, really shouldn't feel this good to be touched,* I thought, echoing my earlier feelings. But if Flor's fingers around my wrist had been like a flame, his body pressed into mine was like the sun.

I arched my back and felt my hips rock against his, felt his erection hot and unyielding against my thigh. I struggled to pull my arms from his grip, to touch him the way his left hand was touching me, sliding down my side, caressing my hip through my skirt. When his fingers met the bare skin of my upper thigh, I gasped into his mouth, felt his tongue dig deeper while my heart split open and released all of the feelings I'd been keeping back for so long.

Butterflies had taken flight in my stomach, battering at my belly with nervous wings and tightening places low in my body, places that I hadn't even realized could ache like this. Oh God, I didn't think *anything* could ever ache so bad and feel so good at the same time. That is, until Flor's fingers found my panties, the black silky ones with the lace that I'd put on just because. A lick of flame raced up my spine as he touched me and I found I could barely breathe, let alone think. I knew my dad and stepmom were upstairs, that finding us like this would destroy them both, but I couldn't stop. I didn't *want* to stop.

Flor pulled back a fraction of an inch, just enough that he could whisper my own name against my lips.

"*Abigail.*"

As quick as it started, it stopped.

"Abi, is that you, honey?" I heard my dad's voice a split second before I snapped my eyes open and found the lights in the stairwell flickering on.

Florian released me, much the same way the guy at the party had, like I was hurting him, burning him too hot, scorching him too deep. Like I was dangerous.

His eyes mirrored back a look of hurt, of longing, that I knew was plastered across my own face. I dropped my arms, crossed them over my chest. Ice was seeping into me at that look, at this taboo breath that was passing between us. We both knew we couldn't have what we wanted, and that we never could. I reached out, just once, a single hand grasping for a love I knew could be, but Florian didn't reach back. Instead, he backed up, chest rising and falling with rapid breath, his lips still moist from the touch of my own. And then he turned toward the front door and left. Just like that.

"Yeah, Dad," I called back, fighting to keep my voice strong and steady. I didn't want him to find me down here like this, panting and red cheeked and moist lipped and … hurting. I slid to the floor as tears stung my eyes again. "I'll be right up." I put my forehead against my arm and waited for the emotions to pass.

But they never did.

And Flor never touched me again.

We never even spoke of it.

CHAPTER ONE

I set the box down on the counter and eyed Flor's ass as he bent over and set a second, much smaller box on the floor with little care or consideration as to what was inside. I didn't mind scoping him out anymore. I had long given up on anything happening between us. I mean, our parents were head over heels in *loco* love with one another and they even referred to us as "their kids". It would kill them if they even knew I thought my stepbrother was hot.

"Um, hello," I said, knowing the exact look Flor was going to toss over his shoulder. *Ah ha! I was right; it's a scowl.* "It says *fragile* on it. It also says *bedroom*." I put one hand on my hip and smirked, knowing how frustrated I was making him, forcing him to carry the smallest boxes while I shouldered the largest ones. Call it a case of raging feminism or what have you, but I liked pissing him off. Big tough guy that he was, I let him carry in the pillows and the lamps while I hauled in the pots and pans, the kitchen stools, and the boxes of books – with great glee, mind you.

"How the hell was I supposed to know?" he said, letting his scowl relax into a smirk as he leaned back against the counter. "Maybe it said *fra-gee-lay*. I thought it was fucking Italian." He stood up suddenly and snapped his fingers, breezing past me before I could get out another word, make fun of him for his infatuation with a *A Christmas Story*. I decided to follow after him and try anyway.

"Can't even come up with your own jokes?" I asked, following quickly behind Florian and down the steps to the street. I don't know what was putting the pep in my step – the fact that I got my first place or the fact that I could tell I was getting under Flor's skin. "Have to pull material from old movies? That's pretty sad there, Flor. How do the girls at the shop take that? Or are they even cultured enough to know what *A Christmas Story* is?" I hated mentioning the girls at my stepbrother's tattoo studio, even as a joke, but Flor's 'groupies' were a fact of life that I'd since learned to deal with. *Each one like a thorn in my side,* I thought as I continued to scope out his ass. It was watch from afar or do nothing at all. At this point, the absence of Florian in my life hurt more than his distanced presence.

Flor climbed into the back of the moving truck and grabbed a box before pausing and glancing over his shoulder at me. I noticed it was a heavy one and stepped up, putting my arms out like I thought he was trying to hand it to me. He scowled again and I smiled.

"What do you take me for?" he asked, raising his dark brows in a way that made my toes curl. "An idiot? That's my pre-sex question right there. Tell me about the leg lamp or I don't take you home tonight. Works like a charm."

"Oh, I'm sure it does," I replied, smothering the surge of jealousy that threatened to take over me and kill my mood. Flor and girls and … sex. This was yet another thing I'd learned to deal with. I wasn't his, and he wasn't mine. We could never belong to one another and much as I fantasized about him staying celibate for me, pining over me every waking day and night, it wasn't going to happen. I was a big girl; I knew that and I could handle it. Or at least I thought I could.

I took a deep breath and smoothed a hand over my curls, hoping they hadn't already dissolved to stray strands of fluff in the blustery afternoon air. Addison was going to be here any minute, dragging her longtime boyfriend and *his* brother along for the ride. She'd promised me this one was cute, tall enough to wear heels with, and had a brain at least three times the size of my brother's. "I bet they just can't wait to dive into bed with an underdeveloped boy who still watches his favorite Christmas movie every night before bed."

"Not every night," Flor said, pulling the box from the truck and purposely sidestepping around me. He leaned in and breathed hot breath against my ear, making me shiver. "Just on weekends. And who said I was underdeveloped?" I kicked him lightly with my bare foot and climbed into the truck, searching for a very specific box that had somehow gotten lost in the fray. Inside was my long ago dismantled shrine to my stepbrother: a series of pictures and notes and gifts that he'd given me over the years. I used to keep it all in one of the bottom drawers of my dresser, but after … the 'incident' as I liked to refer to it, I put it all away in a box, taped it up and hadn't looked at it since. Unfortunately, it had somehow ended up on the truck even though I'd meant to throw it away. For three years it had sat on the top shelf of my closet collecting dust. I was lucky the bastard never found it, nosy little asshole that he was. Once, I'd come home to find him sitting on the edge of my bed, an unlit cigarette between his lips, and a condom I'd gotten from my sex ed class clutched between two of his fingers. It had taken me an entire hour to convince him that I was actually still a virgin, not that it should've been any of his business anyway.

I felt a frown crease my lips as various Florian flavored anecdotes flashed through my memory, several of which involved Flor's bare ass as he screwed whoever happened to be the flavor of the week. *Why could he never manage to close his damn door?!* I wondered as a hot flush lit up my cheeks.

"Boo!"

I nearly jumped out of my skin, spinning to find Addi standing on the street with her hair in pigtails and her shirtsleeves rolled up, ready to move her stuff into our new place. Even dressed as practically as she was, she was still stylish in a way I could never be – partially thanks to her longterm friendship with a drag queen named Theo. That man was the epitome of glamour and, although I might not ever admit it, I was horribly jealous of his ass. It wasn't fair for a man to be so much prettier than me.

I clutched a hand to my chest to still my beating heart and felt a grin split my lips. Here I was, knocked out of my reverie by the best friend I hadn't seen in person more than a half dozen times in the last few years. With Instagram, Skype, and Facebook however, it didn't feel like it'd been more than fifteen minutes. Probably because it hadn't. Pretty sure I'd snapped a photo of Flor's ass and texted it to her when we'd first gotten here, not that she appreciated him the way I did. Honestly, I was actually a little suspicious that she wished him an untimely death at the jaws of rabid wolves.

"Addi!" I squealed as she climbed into the truck and we proceeded to squeeze the life out of one another. She always seemed to bring out the kid in me, something I desperately needed. It didn't take Flor's constant nagging to remind myself that I could be a little too serious sometimes.

I pulled back and grinned at my best friend who returned the smile, holding my hands in hers as we passed silent signals to one another. *We're finally out. We have our own place. This is going to be fucking awesome.* I think I also detected a slight twitch of her brow and a little, *you better not still be on about that, bitch* in regards to Florian, but I couldn't be sure. Maybe I was projecting? "I cannot even believe you're here." The words came out in a rush as I tilted my head back and stared up at the rusted white ceiling of the moving truck. *No more hanging out with people I can barely stand, who use me to hang out with my brother, just so I can have a social circle.* The thought that some of those same said people were going to the community college instead of to the university with me didn't escape my notice.

It wasn't that I was reveling in being better than them, only that I knew how lazy most of them had gotten the last few years of high school.

"You better believe it," she said, pulling her hands from mine and poking me playfully in the shoulder. "Because I just drove halfway across the country to go to school with your ass – and be an Oregon *Duck.*" Addi shivered, not at all impressed by our university's stellar football team. The only kudos she would grant them was that they'd made a pretty awesome parody video of Psy's song, *Gangnam Style.* "Now. Show me our new place, Abigail Sharp, or more specifically, the bathroom. I have got to *piss* like a racehorse."

"Classy, Addi," I said as I swept past her, still surreptitiously looking for the missing box. If Flor found it before I did, I could be in for a world of trouble; I'd never hear the end of it from him. "Nice to know you've matured well beyond the foulmouthed fifteen year old you once were." I gave her a wink while she simultaneously flipped me off, and jumped from the back of the truck, pausing to examine the two men waiting a respectful distance away from us. Addi climbed down next to me and elbowed me in the side with a Flor-worthy smirk plastered across her full mouth.

"What do you think?" she whispered, raising a dark brow and running her tongue along her lower lip as she gazed through lovestruck eyes at the man in the short sleeved white button-down. He had red curly hair and skin as milky white and pale as Addi's was rich and brown. I sat somewhere in between with skin the color of a really good caramel macchiato from Starbucks – with just a dash of extra cream.

Or maybe that was my mind fantasizing about coffee again. Flor and I had yet to find the coffee maker his mother had bought for me and proudly loaded on the truck herself. She was as happy for me to start my life as she'd been for her own son. It made me feel almost guilty for checking out his beautiful butt no less than three times today.

"He's … " I struggled for the right word to describe Patrick Browne and decided an overly analytical dissertation on the looks of Addi's boyfriend would not be appropriate. *I need to get out more.* Luckily, Addi's arrival would pretty much guarantee that. "Gorgeous, babe," I told her, examining the splotch of freckles across her beloved's nose, and the way his skinny arms struggled with a box marked *heavy as shit* in scrawling black Sharpie. Okay, so maybe *gorgeous* wasn't exactly the right word, but what was I going to tell my best friend about the love of her life? I'd seen plenty of pictures of him and had always managed to avoid commenting on his looks. *I'm such a shallow bitch,* I thought as I smiled and wished I didn't have Florian around to compare every Tom, Dick, and Harry against. I decided to let my comment stand as is and moved on to checking out her boyfriend's brother when Flor stepped in front of me, arms crossed and smirking.

"Hey Addi," he said, giving her a friendly hug, that stupid smirk still stuck to his lips. "Hope your trip didn't suck too much dick." I cringed at Flor's crudeness, but at least I knew Addi was used to it. She looked Flor up and down and then smiled, not at all interested in him. It was one of the reasons we'd stayed so close all these years: she was one of the few girls I'd ever met who hadn't developed a crush on my stepbrother, and wasn't using me to get close to him. I knew for a fact that she didn't even find him attractive. For whatever reason, skinny Irish boys had always been Addi's thing. Maybe it was the accent? "Or should I say, hope *you* didn't suck too much dick during your trip." He nodded his chin at Addi's boyfriend, Patrick, and his brother.

"Nice to see you, too, Flor," she said evenly, "and nice to see you're still an annoying asshole." The two of them stared at each other for several long moments, the bad blood between them sizzling in the gentle autumn sunshine. Addi let her eyes swing over to mine. She knew how I'd once felt about him, even knew about the shrine and the missing box. And she'd never judged me for it, not once. I loved her for that. "Let me get the guys over here, so we can get the introductions out of the way. They're both shy by nature, so it might be awkward." She paused to give me another look, opening her brown eyes wide enough that I knew I was supposed to pay attention. The fact that they were rimmed in bright blue and silver eyeshadow didn't hurt either. "Just give 'em both a chance for me, okay?"

I nodded and Addi moved away to grab them. She knew how picky I was when it came to men. I tried not to pretend that growing up around someone like Florian hadn't gone and screwed it all up for me. He was tall and muscular, with full lips and hair as soft as silk that he barely styled but always managed to look good anyway. The scar on his chin was – for whatever reason – a big turn on for me and the myriad piercings and tattoos he'd collected over the years didn't hurt either. Plus, he worked at a tattoo shop and inked skin for a living. Somehow, football stars and science nerds and bankers and even CEOs ... none of that did it for me. I think Flor, in our many years living together, had somehow infected me with this dangerous, funky streak that I didn't know how to express.

"She's setting you up?" he asked, face all a-scowl again. "On your moving day? What if this guy is a freak and he starts stalking you or something?" I ignored my brother's overprotective urges and tried to keep my mind from correcting me. *Step. Stepbrother. Not brother.* As if I needed to be reminded.

I reached back and scooped my hair into a messy ponytail, snapping a hair tie from around my wrist to hold it in place. Sweat was already beading on the back of my neck and my palms were moist with nervous energy. I closed my eyes for a brief second, pretending Flor's body heat wasn't warm and comforting against my right arm.

"This guy is Addi's boyfriend's brother. She's known him for three years, Flor. Back off." I opened my eyes, plastered a welcoming smile on my face and moved forward to meet the guy. Flor's hand on my upper arm froze me in place. He'd been careful, ridiculously careful, not to touch me since the night we shared our single and only kiss. And I mean *careful.* He didn't push me playfully anymore after that, didn't grab my arm to stop me from leaving during a fight, didn't even let his leg brush mine when we sat in the back of a car together.

I looked over at him with a puzzled expression and found the same mirrored on his perfect face. He dropped his hand and stepped back.

"Abigail," Addi said, drawing my attention back around. I was sure my pupils were huge and my lips parted, that I looked half-paralyzed with the emotions that were boiling up in my belly. Well, maybe not emotions. Maybe they were hormones and maybe, just maybe, they weren't from my belly, but my — "This is Patrick's brother, Dorian." I reached out a hand, letting my eyes meet the new guy's. They were green, like Flor's, but not as intense, more like a new sprout than the thorn of a rose. *I want to get punctured; I want to bleed.*

I swallowed back the dark thoughts swirling in my brain.

"Nice to meet you," we said in unison and then smiled shyly. Flor was suddenly there at my shoulder, ruining the moment like he'd done so many other times with other boys. I swear, after that night, that kiss, he took up the brother mantle and he ran the gauntlet with it. He intimidated new dates, threatened exes, and essentially made my dating life a living hell. I was even under the suspicion that he still thought I was a virgin.

Dorian glanced over at my stepbrother, his pale throat moving in a nervous swallow as he released my hand and reached out for Flor's. The two men stared at each other for a long moment before Flor put a wicked smile on his face and shook his hand.

"How's it going?" he asked, like he actually cared — which I knew for a fact that he didn't, not unless this guy's intentions had anything to do with getting me into bed. And then his only mission was to make sure that didn't happen. I appreciated the idea that he cared enough to take an interest, but it felt like too little, too late. His familial concern did nothing to replace that empty, icy ache he'd left me with. "I'm Abi's brother."

"Stepbrother," I corrected while Addi rolled her eyes to the frigid autumn sky.

"They've been living together since they were five," she told Dorian, wrinkling her nose a bit at the nervous beads of sweat popping up on the man's pale forehead. He had bright red hair, like his brother, and thin pink lips. But, unlike his younger sibling, he had nicely muscled arms, a wide sexy chest and an obvious six pack.

"Since Abi was five; I was eight," Flor corrected and then turned away, satisfied that he'd screwed up the meeting well enough that Dorian wouldn't even consider asking me out on a date. I narrowed my eyes as I watched him hop back into the truck and then turned back to Dorian, reaching out to loop my arm through his.

"Can I get you something to drink?" I asked, guiding him towards the steps to our apartment. "I ran to the grocery store this morning and stocked the fridge full of stuff. If you want it, I probably have it."

Dorian cast yet another glance towards Flor and then smiled down at me, letting me guide him into my new house and my new life.

Whether Flor liked it or not.

AVAILABLE ONLINE AT: AMAZON, BARNES & NOBLE, ITUNES, KOBO AND GOOGLE PLAY

IF YOU ENJOYED THIS BOOK
TRY THESE OTHER GREAT TITLES BY
C.M. STUNICH

ABOUT THE AUTHOR

C.M. Stunich is a self-admitted bibliophile with a love for exotic teas and a whole host of characters who live full time inside the strange, swirling vortex of her thoughts. Some folks might call this crazy, but Caitlin Morgan doesn't mind – especially considering she has to write biographies in the third person. Oh, and half the host of characters in her head are searing hot bad boys with dirty mouths and skillful hands (among other things). If being crazy means hanging out with them everyday, C.M. has decided to have herself committed.

She hates tapioca pudding, loves to binge on cheesy horror movies, and is a slave to many cats. When she's not vacuuming fur off of her couch, C.M. can be found with her nose buried in a book or her eyes glued to a computer screen. She's the author of over thirty novels – romance, new adult, fantasy, and young adult included. Please, come and join her inside her crazy. There's a heck of a lot to do there.

Oh, and Caitlin loves to chat (incessantly), so feel free to e-mail her, send her a Facebook message, or put up smoke signals. She's already looking forward to it.

www.cmstunich.com, www.facebook.com/cmstunichauthor,
twitter.com/cmstunich, www.goodreads.com/cmstunich

45683436R20157

Made in the USA
San Bernardino, CA
18 February 2017